Riding Lessons

Riding Lessons

AN ELLEN & NED BOOK

 1

JANE SMILEY

A YEARLING BOOK

This is a work of fiction. Names, characters, places, and incidents either are the product of the author's imagination or are used fictitiously. Any resemblance to actual persons, living or dead, events, or locales is entirely coincidental.

Text copyright © 2018 by Jane Smiley
Cover art copyright © 2018 by AG Ford

All rights reserved. Published in the United States by Yearling, an imprint of Random House Children's Books, a division of Penguin Random House LLC, New York. Originally published in hardcover in the United States by Alfred A. Knopf, an imprint of Random House Children's Books, a division of Penguin Random House LLC, New York, in 2018.

Yearling and the jumping horse design are registered trademarks of Penguin Random House LLC.

Visit us on the Web! rhcbooks.com

Educators and librarians, for a variety of teaching tools, visit us at RHTeachersLibrarians.com

Library of Congress Cataloging-in-Publication Data is available upon request.

ISBN 978-1-5247-1814-5 (paperback)

Printed in the United States of America
10 9 8 7 6 5 4 3 2 1
First Yearling Edition 2019

Chapter 1

Tonight my mom said, "Ellen Leinsdorf, do you lie in bed and plan about how to be naughty?" So now I am lying in bed, and I am thinking about that, and I guess what I always plan is two things—how to get my own horse and how to be funny. The problem with my plans is that they never work out. I have tried wishes, too, but I gave up on that right after third grade. Here is what happened. Last summer, I was down the street at Paulie Miller's birthday party. First, I got in trouble because when I counted the candles on his cake, there were only nine, so I said to Mrs. Miller, "Where's the one to grow on?" but she didn't hear me, so I said it a little louder, *"Where's the one to grow on?* He can't get to ten without it," and she told me to hush, so I hushed. I really did hush. So Paulie closed his eyes and made a wish (you could see it in his face), and blew out the candles. He only blew out eight, and I saw his mom blow out the last one. But still I hushed because she gave me a look.

Supposedly, your wish is a secret, but Paulie had no secrets. I knew he was going to wish for a Creepy Crawlers set, because that's what he told me the day before when we were talking about the party. I told him that your wish had to be a secret and that you had to wish for something good, like people not going hungry or plenty of rain right when we need it, but his face got this look, and he said, "Well, I want Creepy Crawlers."

After we ate the cake and the ice cream (the cake was vanilla, with vanilla icing, and good; the ice cream was chocolate—yuck), everyone went outside to run around and play statues and then dodgeball, and I knew what I had to do. I went to the pile of presents and took the one that was the Creepy Crawlers set (big box, and anyway, I could see the words through the tissue paper) and I put it in the closet, under a lot of stuff. It didn't take me very long, and then I closed the door of the closet and went out and played with the other kids. I am really good at statues.

We came in and had some jelly beans and sat down to open the presents, and Paulie got an Erector set, a baseball bat, a ball, a Frisbee, two books, and some watercolors and a pad (from me—Mom always says to give as a present what you yourself like best; I told him I would teach him how to draw a horse). But then his mom began running around, looking behind stuff and under the couch and all, and at first I didn't know what was going on, and then I realized that she was looking for the Creepy Crawlers, but I didn't say anything. And they never found it until the rains started in the fall and they had to get out their boots and raincoats. I had hidden it really well. Whenever I do something, I make my best effort, just like Mom tells me.

Even though I didn't get in trouble, I did realize that if you keep your wish a secret, you probably won't get it, so you have to say what you wish and then, probably, say it again and again, because that's the only way it works, even if it takes a long time to work.

Every weekend and sometimes more often than that, I go to the stables and have a riding lesson. My teacher is Abby Lovitt. She is in high school, and she is a really good rider. The horse I ride every weekend is one she trained whose name is True Blue. We call him

Blue. Last year, I rode a pony, but he got sold. Blue is a lot bigger, and at first I was afraid of how tall he is, but then I got on him and he was so nice, much nicer than the pony, and now I like him very much. The pony wasn't bad, but he was a lot like me. The pony was always saying, "I will do what I want, and you can come along for the ride," and then he would toss his head, and lucky for me, mostly he wanted to do what I wanted him to, but not always. Blue says, "What do you want to do? That is what I want to do, too."

Grown-ups will tell you that horses can't talk. It might be that Todd Kerrigan, who is in my class and who I eat lunch with every day, is the only person in the world who thinks that the horse on TV, Mr. Ed, is actually talking. I used to watch *Mr. Ed,* say, two years ago, but when I started taking riding lessons, I decided that I was not interested in a horse who just stands around in a stall, moving his mouth to a voice-over. Anyway, my dad says that *Mr. Ed* isn't on TV anymore, so I guess that was why last month Todd finally stopped asking me if I had seen *Mr. Ed* the night before. Abby might say that horses don't talk, too, but she talks to the horses all the time, and why would she do that if the horses don't talk back to her? I mean,

I'm not talking about what everyone knows—if someone is walking toward Blue's stall and shouts, "Blue, Blue! How are you?" he will pop his head out and whinny. That makes everyone laugh, and then you are supposed to think that he is saying, "I am fine. How are you?" because he has *very good manners*. My mom talks to me about manners all the time. "Please" and "Thank you" and "How do you do? Nice to meet you," and shake hands and look the person in the eye, and if she wants to give you a little kiss on the cheek, stand there quietly, and don't wipe it off, if you must, until she has turned away. (This is my aunt Louise, and Mom swears that there isn't a yellow cloud of perfume all around her head, but I see it and it makes me kind of dizzy. Every time I tell Mom this, she says that I am exaggerating again.) At school, of course, you are supposed to sit quietly in your seat, and raise your hand when you know the answer, and *do not wave it back and forth* just because you know the answer and no one else does, and no one has known the answer for the last three questions, so why does Miss Cranfield have to keep calling on them? It is a waste of time, but the more you know the answer, the less they call on you, and so how is that good manners?

Anyway, if I can possibly be quiet (and sometimes I possibly can), I sit on the fence and listen to Abby talking to Blue or Gee Whiz or one of Jane's horses, and she says, "Oh, that is very good! Nice square turn, now easy up into the canter, right lead. Good boy. Four strides to the crossbar, ease back now, one two three four. Good jump. Let's try that again." I'm not saying that she talks to them all the time—you can't in a horse show, for one thing, and for another, all conversations stop and start. But maybe they are saying to her, "Did you like that? What now? Which lead? Tell me the difference between right and left again . . . oh yes, I've got it. One two three four, two plus two is four, this crossbar is easy as pie, let's try another one."

Blue and Gee Whiz are both grays, and both Thoroughbreds, but everything else about them is different. Blue is always looking around. He notices things, and he sometimes doesn't like what he notices. I would say that he is a little shy, but Jane says "careful" is the word. When I am riding him, I am supposed to let him take his time. He may look and make up his mind, and if we don't push him, he will go on and do what he is told. He is a very beautiful horse, dark mane, dark tail, and dapples along his underside and over his haunches. When he first came to the stables where I ride (he used to be Abby's and he lived at her place, but since my ears are very big, I know from *eavesdropping* that Jane bought him, also for a lot of money, but my ears are not big enough to know how much), he was very spooky, but Jane says that Abby has performed a miracle with that horse, and now he is very reliable, which is a good thing, because my mom would make me stop riding him if he acted bad. Jane runs the stables, which are big and very expensive, and surrounded by a famous golf course. Lots of people board their horses there, and they have horse shows and golf tournaments.

Gee Whiz is huge and very white. He used to be a racehorse and won a lot of money, but Abby didn't get any of it because she didn't own him in those days. He stares at things, and does not seem to be afraid of anything. He lives at Abby's ranch (Oak Valley Ranch, it is called) and only comes to the stables to school over bigger fences. If he comes on a day when I am having a lesson, I try to stay after my lesson and watch. Abby and Jane always talk about whether to go slow with him, because they don't want to overdo it, but I am here to tell you that the last thing on earth that Gee

Whiz wants to do is to go slow. He wants to go fast and jump big jumps, and I admit that yes, he needs to learn to turn a little better. Blue is much more handy. "Handy" is a word that I really like. In every horse show, they have a class called Handy Hunters, where the horse has to do all kinds of things, some at the trot, some at the canter, some at the hand gallop, tight turns, halts, opening gates. When I get to jump higher than a foot and a half and go in hunter classes (maybe next year), that is what I want to do. My mom says she does not see how we will be able to afford much showing, because showing is really expensive.

Abby has another horse, too, a racehorse. His name is Jack So Far, and he is down in Los Angeles. He was born on the Lovitts' ranch, and his mom died when he was a foal. He is getting ready for his first race, which should happen in the next few weeks, according to Jane. He was training at Vista del Canada, which is a pretty nice place near here, but he went to LA after a few months, and I heard Jane ask Abby if she was going to go to the race, but even though I made my ears as big as I possibly could, I did not hear what Abby answered, so I do not know. And now I can see a shadow under the door of my room, and then there is a little creak, which means that Mom is peeking in to make sure I am asleep, and so I close my eyes and let my head sort of flop to one side, and I do those slow breaths so she will think I'm asleep and go to bed. It is ten o'clock; my bedtime is eight-thirty, and I have to get up at seven, so I guess I really should go to sleep.

Chapter 2

We live right down from my school. If I walk, it is four minutes (Mom gave me a watch for Christmas, and I have taken very good care of it). If I run, it is two, because I have to run uphill. But sometimes, like today, when the fog is out and the sky is clear, I walk backward. Today it took ten minutes. I was looking down the hill to where the street disappears, and then I saw a few roofs of houses, and beyond that, there was the line of the ocean shading into the mountains across the bay, ending halfway up the sky, darker blue against lighter blue. I know you can't see dolphins or whales jumping from five blocks up, even if you are farsighted, but I looked for them anyway. I didn't get to school until after the first bell, and then I ran to my room, number four, down the hall to the right on the first floor. I sat down at my desk and looked out the window at a few trees. I do wish that Miss Cranfield's classroom were on the top floor, or even on the roof, because I would like to look over the trees and watch the ocean while the other kids are trying to figure out how to answer her questions. At least, it would be something to do. While she was taking the roll, I stared at the letters of the alphabet that run along the top of the blackboard. I can say the alphabet backward. It is easy. There are twenty-six letters in the alphabet. You tap a finger with each letter—thumb, Z; forefinger, Y; middle finger, X; ring finger, W; baby finger, V—all the way back to A. If you get there without forgetting a letter, the A is by itself. Generally, if I am going to forget a letter, it will be I. I don't know why that is. Also, the middle letters of the alphabet are M and N. I think there should be another letter between them—the exact middle. It would be the *ch* sound so you wouldn't have to write two letters to make one sound. These are the things I think about at school while the other kids are trying to get their work done. Sometimes my dad says that I am too smart for my own good. Also, I reminded myself that today is Friday, my favorite day of the week—tomorrow is my riding lesson, and if today is nice, tomorrow will probably be nice, too. We have had plenty of rain this spring, but I am hoping that is over.

Dad sells vacuum cleaners. He's gone from Monday to Thursday, because he has to go to people's houses and demonstrate the vacuum cleaners on the floors and the carpets that the people actually have. On Fridays and Saturdays, Mom works the evening shift at the department store. I don't have to say which one, because there is only one, and it is really big. Maybe Mom doesn't have to work there, but she has been working there since she was in high school, and she gets a discount, and anyway, it is the most beautiful place in town, and it is only a short walk, so why not go there? I don't know if she will keep working there after the baby is born, though.

No one has told me about the baby, but whisper whisper whisper, and Mom in the attic rummaging around, and on Wednesday I found a book about baby names inside the drawer of the table beside her bed. However, I don't say anything. Being about to have a baby is no big deal on our block, and anyway, if you are an only child, everyone thinks you are spoiled rotten and always get your way. You do not. If you are an only child, you cannot get away with anything, be-cause someone is watching. The Murphys live down the street. They have seven kids, from thirteen down to four. The two oldest are girls, Mary and Jane, and the rest are boys. Mary and Jane do everything they are supposed to, including help cook dinner every night, and the boys do whatever they want, right on down to Brian, the four-year-old, whose favorite game is squatting on the curb and dropping leaves and sticks into the street. If it's raining, he likes to see them float down the street. If it's not raining, I don't know what in the world he is doing, but not a single Murphy seems to realize that he could step off the curb anytime. Jimmy Murphy is in my class. If he has ever raised his hand, I can't remember it, but he is great with spit-balls. Just today, during arithmetic, Miss Cranfield turned to write a bunch of multiplication problems on the board, and he hit Lucy Morgan, Frankie Crandall, and Maria Rodriguez. He has hit me once or twice, but I think it is funny, so I don't mind. At lunch, I traded him my egg salad sandwich for his peanut but-ter and orange marmalade sandwich. He also talked Annie Parks out of her Milky Way. I could go home for lunch, we live so close, but if I go home, I have to eat things I don't like, and if I stay here, I get to eat things I do like, like chocolate milk from a little carton and peanut butter and Juicy Fruit gum, something Lizzie Conrad always has, and will give you for a nickel— one stick for a nickel, even though at the drugstore, a whole package costs a nickel. But if you don't pay her her nickel, she says, "Fine, go to the drugstore." She is in fifth grade. On the playground, she makes the nickels in her pocket rattle as she is walking around. I've thought about doing this as a way to get the money to buy a horse, but I don't think Lizzie would let me.

After lunch, we have reading. I'm in the highest reading group, and so we don't have to read what the other kids are reading. There are three of us, and we are reading chapter ten of *The Borrowers*. My mom used to read this to me, so I know the story, but there are some big words in it, and it is way better than *Dick and Jane,* so it's fine with me. I told Miss Cranfield that we should read *The Black Stallion* next, and she said that she would think about it. After that, *National Velvet.* I would like to write a book, but I am left-handed, and my writing isn't very good. It would take me way too long to write everything that I think, so what I do is, I think my book. I tell my story to myself as I am walking to school, or sitting at my desk, or riding in the car, or lying in bed, and I tell it so many times to myself that I remember it perfectly.

It used to be that Rodney would have my horse ready when I got to the stables. Rodney is funny, and he likes to tease me. He does things like take off his hat and bow to me. He says, "Yes, madam," in a silly accent, which makes me laugh. The other great thing about Rodney is that he is short, and he told me that a long time ago he was a jockey. He says that soon we will see eye to eye. But Jane and Mom and Abby decided that I "need to learn a few things," so when we got there Saturday (Dad drove me again—Mom didn't even get up to make breakfast), I had to do brushing and hoof-picking and tacking up. Blue is very good about putting his head down to take the bit, so that part was easy. I guess Abby trained him by holding out a lump of sugar, then giving it to him after the bit was in his mouth. Rodney put on the saddle and tightened the girth, but I had to put my finger between the girth and Blue's side and feel how tight it was. Then I had to mount him myself. I did it Rodney's way—I led Blue over to the fence, told him to stand, and then climbed the fence and hoped for the best. When I looked down between me and Blue, it did seem like a long way to the ground. But he stood quietly, just gazing a little at Abby, who was in the middle of the arena. Yes, I was talking the whole time. I always talk the whole time, because I'm so happy to be there, to be getting on Blue, to know that since Dad brought me and not Mom, I will do some jumping and not in secret. I can talk and plan at the same time. It is easy.

It was a little windy—a nice enough day, but not a really nice day. There are trees all around the stables, and the fog seemed to be caught in the tops of the trees, as if it wanted to go out, but couldn't. There was a horse in the big arena having some kind of lesson over big jumps, and right when we came into the turn going toward that arena, the horse bucked, kicked out, and dumped his rider—her legs made a scissors and her arms flew out, and she landed upside down. Blue turned his head, and I know that he said, "Why in the world would any horse do that? He must be a very bad horse. I would never do that." Abby had me halt, and then she came over to the fence, and we watched for a minute until the rider got up and brushed her hands down over her breeches and walked to her horse, who was standing in the center of the arena, and got back on. I asked who the rider was, and Abby said that it was her friend Sophia, riding a fancy horse named Pie in the Sky, who Abby had been riding in the summer. Then I remembered seeing Sophia, Sophia Rosebury, a lot. We watched her and the horse go up into the canter, and then jump a bunch of high fences as if nothing bad had ever happened before in her life. Abby looked up at me and said, "Now you have seen why you always should wear a hard hat."

Of course I nodded.

I could tell that Abby was more upset than I was, because she made Blue and me do lots and lots of circles all over the arena, in both directions, and yes, Blue was maybe a bit more edgy after the accident than he had been before, but I believed him. If you are sliding to the right or the left, Blue moves to get underneath you. He does not want you to fall off. Even so, as soon as you start saying these sorts of things about horses, things that you *know*, grown-ups don't even wait until you're finished to start shaking their heads. Horses don't think like that, horses are afraid of the stick and want the carrot, and in *The World Book Encyclopedia* (we have a set of those, because Dad was selling them for a while) it says that horses are stupider than dogs, elephants, and pigs, but I know better. I am sorry, but I do.

Finally, we got to canter, which is a wonderful thing on Blue. After a bunch of circles in both directions, Abby let me go around the whole arena, and Blue just rocked along. My hands were soft, my thumbs were up, my heels were down, and I was looking where I was going. And anyway, the bad horse was led out of the big arena. Blue watched him go, but also just kept cantering.

Dad found himself a cup of coffee somewhere, and he leaned against the fence while I was jumping. The jumps are eighteen inches. Every time I ask Abby to raise them, she says that the most important thing to learn is not height, but steering, and it is true that sometimes I think we are going right to the center of the jump and somehow we do not get there. At least, she set up a real course, with eight fences.

I circled to the right and came to a crossbar, then went down the long side over an in-and-out, then I turned right and crossed the diagonal, jumping a small gate. Then I turned left and went down the other long side over a log and, six strides later, an oxer. Then I circled to the left and turned down the middle, where there was another oxer, and finally, I circled again, jumping the crossbar from the other direction. It was a fun course, and I sort of did a good job. Abby called me to the center and told me to make sure that I could see the middle of the fence between Blue's ears, and also that Blue's ears were pointing toward the fence—*he* has to be looking at it, too. So we went back to the gate and tried again, and this time we both paid attention. I really did not know what else was happening—I just kept looking through his ears, and he kept his ears pointing toward the middle of the jumps. It took a really long time, but then seemed like it was over in a second. I wanted to do it once more, but Abby said no, that you always have to finish with your best ride so that you will look forward to the next one. Dad kept tapping his coffee cup on the top rail of the fence like he was clapping, and Blue told me that I had done a very good job, which is what I told Rodney when I got back to the barn, and Rodney said, "Ya've got a gret future in front of ya, madam," and then we laughed. Because of the weather, Blue was not sweaty, but I did have to lead him around for a while. He walked along behind me. I watched Abby get Gee Whiz ready, but Dad had to get home, so I couldn't stay for her lesson.

When we left, she said, "Next week at our place! Because of the show here!" And so, in spite of how much fun I had had, I was mad about two things—that I didn't get to see her lesson and that I wouldn't be going in the show (too expensive). I'm sure that we are saving money for the baby. I wish they would just tell me the truth.

Chapter 3

Even so, when Dad and I are alone in the car (and he lets me sit in the front seat, which Mom never does), sometimes he tells me things, and today he told me about when he was eleven. He grew up in Pennsylvania. We have gone there three times, twice for Christmas and once in the summer, and Grandma Edith and Grandpa Gordon live in the same house that they always have, a small house on a long road under big maple and oak trees. Anyway, Dad started telling me about how when he was eleven, his favorite thing to do was to hitchhike up that road to the orphans' home, where his friend was named Jimmy Murphy, just like our Jimmy Murphy, and what they would do was go out to the creek that ran along the back of the orphans'-home property, and they would take traps and set them for the beavers. Almost every time they did this, they would catch a beaver, sometimes two, and then they would shoot them in the head with Dad's .22 and skin them. They tacked the skins to some trees to dry, and then they would come back and take the skins down, and there was a man who would buy them for a few dollars and make them into hats or something.

This is exactly the sort of story that Mom would never let Dad tell me if she was around, and really, it is just like that book that Miss Cranfield reads to us at the end of the school day, *My Side of the Mountain*. I kept my mouth shut while Dad was telling this story, because he answered all my questions without me asking—it was okay to kill the beavers because there were too many of them and they were blocking up the creek; Jimmy Murphy was an orphan because his dad had been killed in the war, and then his mom got sick and died; Dad had his own .22 because everyone did. He never shot anything but beavers and squirrels. He was finished telling it around the time we pulled into the driveway, and I realized that now that I had listened to this story, I was not so mad about the horse show and missing Abby riding Gee Whiz. There was grilled ham-and-cheese for lunch, which I really like, and pretty soon I had talked so much about how great my two jumping rounds were that I was in a good mood.

I went outside after lunch and stared down the hill at the ocean. I had Dad's story in my mind all day. I have never even seen an orphanage, except in a movie. I decided to walk around the block and look for one, even though I knew I wouldn't find one, but it gave me something to think about—what if the Jenkinses' house were an orphanage? What if our school were an orphanage? "What" and "if" are my two favorite words, and the next ones after them don't always have to be "I had a horse of my own." You can "What if" anything, and then your mind is busy for the rest of the day, and it even gets into your dreams, because that night, I dreamt that a beaver was in my room, hiding in with my stuffed animals, and every time Dad walked by down the hall, the beaver squeaked. But in my dream, I didn't understand what he was saying.

Here are the things I'm allowed to do on my own: walk over to the market, which is four short blocks and two long ones; walk down the hill to the department store, which is two and a half short blocks; go past the department store to the library, which is four more blocks, but short. I can cross two busy streets, but only at the corners, and I could go to the history museum if I wanted to, but I never do. I can walk on the beach, but I can't go into the water if a grown-up isn't with me, and I can walk to Grandma Lydia's house, which is a little past the library. The kids in our neighborhood play mostly at the school, because no one has a very big yard. There are also parks, but the real truth is that all the boys just run up and down the hills, or else ride their bikes everywhere, and there are plenty of places to go. I have a bike, and I can ride it, but there are so many hills in our town that I don't bother. Once, when I was walking up our hill, here came Charlie Koenig on his three-speed. He worked a lot harder than I did, and didn't go any faster. And I have seen him coast down the hill, and I have seen him shoot out across the big road and nearly get hit by a car more than once. That doesn't make me want to ride my bike, either. I pass the Murphys' house; Mrs. Murphy has a bell that she rings every night at dinnertime, and it is so loud that the rest of us can hear it, too, so we pretty much go home when we hear it.

The next day, I was really glad it wasn't Easter, which was two weeks ago. This year, my dress had a sewn-in petticoat, and there was a spot on my left side that kept pricking me and pricking me, so I got into a lot of trouble for fidgeting. We didn't go to church because Mom was tired and Dad doesn't like church anyway. So I got up and put on regular old pants and a loose shirt, and I was already in a good mood when I opened my bedroom window and heard Mrs. Murphy's bell ringing. It was only eight, so it must have been that the kids had to come in and get dressed for Mass. Some of those Murphys are out by six a.m. Mom and Mrs. Murphy went to the high school at the same time, but Mrs. Murphy was three years older than Mom. Grandma Lydia grew up in the house we live in—Mom's grandparents built it when they first moved here. Grandma Lydia's grandfather's name was Allbones, but when they moved to America from England, they changed it to Albin, which is much less creepy. These are the sorts of things that I really like to know. The house is very small, so Grandma Lydia moved out when she married Grandpa John. Mom grew up on Fountain. Aunt Johanna, who was Grandma Lydia's older sister, lived here until she died, and she left the house to Mom, which is why we live here. Great-aunt Johanna's favorite thing to do was gardening, and she had ninety-two different types of plants growing in the garden. Mom spends her Sundays working there. When I went downstairs, she gave me a waffle and a hard-boiled egg, and then took her cup of coffee out onto the back porch, where she stood, looking at something. Dad was still in bed, but he was awake. He was reading the Sunday paper, which he did until lunchtime. At lunchtime, every Sunday, he walks to the market and buys himself a pastrami sandwich with sauerkraut.

The garden is really small—with all of the plants, there is only room for one garden bench and a little table. Mom sits there every evening and enjoys the fragrances. The window of my room looks down on the garden, and that's the way I like it best—staring at the flowers and the patch of green grass from above. The smells are good, too. The ones I like best are the jasmine, the ceanothus, and the wild roses. In the fall, I help set out the bulbs, and in the late spring, I snip off the seedpods. A garden is a lot of work, but it cannot run away. One time, I imagined that I kept a horse in the garden (that was before I knew how much space a horse likes), but now I don't imagine that. There is no place in our town to keep a horse, and that is that. We used to have a dog, a blond cocker spaniel named

Celesta, but she bit me, Michael Murphy, and my cousin Gloria, who was visiting from Pennsylvania, and so Mom gave her away to an old lady who doesn't have any children or grandchildren, and I had to say good riddance. The dog never came when she was called, and Mom said to me, "Well, now you know what it is like to be constantly telling someone what she should be doing, and to never be listened to." However, she was wrong. I always listen, and I always make up my own mind. That's one of Mom's expressions: "I guess I will have to make up my own mind about that."

According to Grandma Lydia, my very greatest virtue is that I know my own mind. But so does Mom and so does Grandma Lydia. Sometimes when we are at Grandma's house, and Mom tells me to do something, and I say what I think, I can see Grandma smiling and turning away because she doesn't want to get into an argument with Mom, but then later, she will say to me, "It's a good thing for a girl to know her own mind, Ellen, so you stick to your guns." Most Sundays, we have dinner with Grandma Lydia and Grandpa John. Today, Grandma Lydia made a roast chicken with dressing and baked potatoes, and there was her hot milk cake for dessert, with homemade blood-orange sherbet, which she only makes once a year. She made a quart, and we ate it all. Everyone was in a good mood when we walked home after dinner, and I went to bed early, and that is just about the last thing I cared to remember for the next five days, because I couldn't wait for my lesson at Abby's ranch, and I didn't want to think about anything else, and so I didn't, including the time I walked into the kitchen when Mom and Grandma Lydia were doing the dishes, and they were mumbling mumbling mumbling, and as soon as they saw me, they went dead quiet. Maybe they are afraid of the baby. Mom was an only child, too. I wanted to say it is just a baby, everybody has one, but I kept that to myself.

After looking forward to my lesson all week, I knew it was going to be bad as soon as I got to Oak Valley Ranch. In the first place, it took a long time to get there. We left three minutes late because Dad was slow finishing his coffee, and then there was traffic where there wasn't supposed to be traffic and never had been traffic. You couldn't even tell why there was traffic—it got slow with a lot of cars, and then everyone was gone. I don't like it when things have no reason for happening, so I kept asking questions, and then Dad said please could he have a moment's peace, and so I looked at my watch and counted a moment, but then when I asked the next question, he gave me a dirty look, pulled over to the side of the road, and told me to get into the backseat. Which I did. That took another two minutes. Abby was all dressed up in her good riding clothes when I got there, which meant that she was going to the show, and not only riding, but also coaching Melinda and maybe that boy Robert (who doesn't ride Blue yet, as far as I know), which made me think about the show and the fact that I couldn't go in it even though I won a couple of ribbons in the fall, and did a very good job.

The horse that was tacked up for me was one of the mares, and as soon as I went over to her, she pinned her ears. Abby watched while I led her to the mounting block, and the whole time the mare was dragging her feet and making me work for every step and saying, "Why do we have to do this? Who are you? I have other things to attend to." I didn't even know her name, and she wasn't telling me. Finally, Abby gave her a little smack on the rump with her crop, or rather, this short western-type whip she has with two long leather flaps that make a noise when she hits the horse, but don't hurt. The mare stepped up to the mounting block then, but her ears were still pinned. I would have to say that by that time, I was in the sort of mood where I would have been pinning my ears, too. Abby said, "Since we don't have Blue, and Sissy doesn't jump, let's go on a trail ride. You need to do that sometimes, because there are more ways of having fun on a horse than jumping and showing."

Maybe that's true, but if you only ride once a week, then you have to do the most fun thing as often as you can. But I didn't say anything. I wasn't even talking. Abby rode Gee Whiz, which was nice, but I couldn't see him, because she rode behind to keep an eye on me, and probably to give Sissy a smack every now and then. As soon as we left the barn, Sissy put her head down and started eating grass, and when I began pulling on her and kicking her to make her move, she said, "Excuse me, I do not understand what you are getting at." Abby handed me the smacker, and I put the loop around my wrist and held the handle along with my right rein. After that, every time Sissy tried to put her head down, I took the reins in my left hand, then smacked her on the rump with my right—*slap*— and Sissy said, "Oh, for heaven's sake, all right!" and walked along. Abby said I was doing a good job, and everyone had to learn to ride a difficult horse at some point. Not every horse is as agreeable as Blue, and now that I am getting older and taller . . . Abby went on. I stopped listening and looked around. It is very sunny at the ranch, and the hills run away in every direction, as green as they can be. We walked up one pretty steep hill, on a trail that went diagonally from the bottom to the top, and then along the fence line. We could see some black cattle in the distance, both cows and calves, but though we could hear them mooing, they stayed far away.

I had to smack Sissy three times to get her to trot, and even then her trot started out uneven, and she was saying, "I prefer walking, thank you." Finally, Abby and Gee Whiz passed us at a wide point in the trail and trotted on, and Sissy trotted after Gee Whiz, as who wouldn't, the way his hooves sprang off the ground and his tail switched back and forth as though it were made of water. However, trotting Sissy was hard work, and when we finally started walking again, I was plenty tired. We looped down around the lower pasture and headed back home, and it was then that I saw Ned for the first time.

Chapter 4

Ned is a shiny dark bay with no white on him except for one little strip down his nose. He was standing in the gelding pasture, away from the others. Ned was eating his hay, and when we walked by, he lifted his head to look at us, and his ears pricked and he whinnied. He's not a pony, and maybe he's not that small—I didn't get close enough to tell—but if there was ever a horse that looked like a puppy, Ned is the one. His rump is rounded and his neck is arched, and there is just something about his face and his way of standing that is the cutest thing I ever saw in a horse. And then he said, "What are you doing? Where are you going?" and walked over to the fence and whinnied again. We kept walking, but I couldn't stop looking at him. Abby was behind me at this point, and she said, "What are you looking at?" and then, "Oh, that's Ned. He was a racehorse. He came last week." And then she walked along as if a horse is just a horse and you can stop looking at him whenever you want. Right then, Sissy put her head down and started eating, and I pretended that I was trying to get her to walk on, but I wasn't. What I really wanted to do was to jump off and run over and give Ned a hug. Abby said, "She can't do that! You are training her, so you have to give her a smack as soon as she starts, because if she gets even a few bites, then it's worth it for her to try, and the next person who rides her will have a harder time."

So I gave her a smack, and then another one, and then we walked on, but I had a plan. For the last ten minutes of the ride, we went into Abby's arena and did some "flat work," which is just turning and stopping and starting and trotting and walking, and Sissy did finally wake up and do her job, so it was more fun than the trail ride. I watched Ned out of the corner of my eye, and he wandered in our direction, taking bites of grass along the way, but all the time curious, all the time saying, "I want to meet you!" You could tell he was a Thoroughbred just by the way he walked, all smooth and soft but covering a lot of ground, completely different from Gee Whiz, who has the longest legs you can imagine and seems to be powered by a big engine, but related in the way you think that any moment either one of them might just rise off the ground and fly away.

By this time, I was talking on and on, as I usually do, and of course I asked about him, and Abby said that he is a four-year-old, that he had five starts and was in the money three times, but now his racing career is finished. In his last race, he strained a tendon, and so had to take a vacation, but because of what the jockey said, they decided to retire him. What the jockey said was that they were in the front of the pack, coming around the turn, and all of a sudden, Ned spit the bit and stopped trying, let all the other horses pass him, and when they crossed the finish line, he was just cantering along and looking around as though he were on vacation. The jockey was smart enough not to hit him, and when he jumped off, the trainer ran out and felt Ned's legs, and there was a little warmth in the right front, but only a little. A good racehorse, a racehorse who really wants to win, would have ignored whatever happened, and maybe injured himself worse, but Ned is too smart to be a racehorse (Abby and I both laughed at that), and so his job now is to recover from his little injury and try something else and maybe he won't be too smart for that. Abby said, "We'll see. Sometimes they are just too smart for their own good." And she looked right at me.

I walked around while Abby did a few things with Gee Whiz. He isn't ready to show yet—she has only been jumping him for two months. He needs about ten million more circles to the left and the right and a lot of backing up and a lot of stepping over to make him pay attention and not take the bit in his mouth and do it his way. He was a racehorse for seven years and won a lot of money and ran in dozens of races, and so, according to Abby, he thinks he knows everything, and sometimes he gallops so fast that she gets tears in her eyes from the speed and starts feeling like she is on a train. He needs to learn that he doesn't have to do that anymore, but Abby likes him so much that she is ready to take the time, and she said, "Anyway, Blue spoiled me rotten, and so I have to get over that."

After we got off and untacked the horses and brushed them down and led them to their pastures, Abby handed me half a carrot and said, "Hide it," and we walked over to the fence, a few yards from where Ned was grazing. Abby put her hand on my shoulder and whispered, "Just wait. Don't do anything." And so we waited. I held the carrot next to my leg on the side away from Ned. The first thing Ned did was look at us, ears pricked. His mane kind of stands up and his forelock is short. He flicked his ears, then went back to eating grass, or rather, to eating some wildflowers that were in the grass. He picked them out very thoroughly, as if he were cleaning his plate. When he was finished, he snorted and looked at us. He wasn't talking to me. Finally, he stepped toward us, as if he had nothing better to do. Abby didn't offer her carrot, so I didn't offer mine. She said, "If he comes to us without us offering him anything, then that means he's been treated kindly." He got to us, paused, then put his head over the fence. Abby lifted her hand and ran her fingers gently around first one eye and then the other eye, and said, "Hello, Ned." She moved back half a step. I reached up and did the same. The hair on his face was smooth and silky. After I had done it for a minute, he closed his eyes and let out some air. Then Abby put her hand under his mane and petted him down the neck. Finally, we gave him the carrot halves. As she was giving him her half, Abby petted the side of his nose first and then slowly brought the carrot up to his lips. If he reached too quickly, she pulled her hand away but didn't stop petting the side of his nose. The second time, he was more careful, stretched his upper lip and took the carrot politely. When I offered him my carrot, I did the same thing, and I could feel the fuzzy warmth of his lip on the palm of my hand. After the carrots were gone, we petted his cheeks and his nose and his neck. Abby said, "The only thing I've really done to train him so far is stand on both sides of him and pet him from his face to his tail until he either puts his head down or walks away. Usually, he puts his head down and I'm the one to walk away. I think that's a good sign."

I thought all of this was incredibly relaxing, and I was ready to lie down in the grass and take a nap. But out of the corner of my eye, I could see Dad standing by the barn with his hands on his hips, and I knew that he wanted to go home and have his lunch and, furthermore, that it is a long drive. By the time we were in the car, backing around to head out of Oak Valley Ranch, I had pretty much forgotten about my ride on Sissy, and was thinking only of Ned.

When I went to bed that night, and Mom asked me when she was tucking me in how my lesson was, I even said that it was great before I remembered that it wasn't great. But anyway.

I, of course, did not take a picture of Ned because Dad didn't bring his camera, but in school on Monday, after I finished my division problems, instead of doing my backward alphabet to pass the time, I turned over my answer sheet and drew two pictures of Ned's head and neck. The second one was better than the first, but I thought the first one had a better eye. Then, of course, we had to pass our papers to the end of the row, but Miss Cranfield is pretty nice, and I thought she wouldn't mind the pictures. She might even like them because they would be a break from the boredom of checking division answers. I also didn't mind turning them in, because I knew that when I got them back on Wednesday, I would be able to see if the ones I had drawn between now and then had gotten better or not.

Here are my favorite things for dinner—minute steak with gravy, mashed potatoes, broccoli with browned butter, homemade rolls, and lemon tarts from the bakery. That night, we had all of those, and also Mom put a cloth on the table and a little vase of some tulips from the garden. It had been sunny all day, and Mom was in a good mood. I thought this was because Dad had decided to put off going out on the road until Tuesday morning, which he sometimes does if he's had a good week the week before. But really, they were softening me up, as if I didn't know what was going on, getting me in a good mood. When I was eating my lemon tart, Mom said, "Ellen, we have something to tell you," and I did not say, "Yes, I know you are going to have a baby," because if I did, then I would have to say that I had seen the baby name book in her drawer, because I opened it looking for a safety pin.

Dad cleared his throat, and they both sat there smiling, and I ate two more bites of my lemon tart, and Mom said, "You are hungry tonight! Good for you!"

So I smiled and said that the mashed potatoes were really yummy. Just as I pressed the edge of my fork into the last part of the lemon tart, Mom said, "We want to tell you something. That you are going to have a sister." Then Mom and Dad looked at each other, and I had one-half of a thought—how did she know already that the baby was a girl?—and then Dad said, "There is something else we have to tell you, and maybe we should have told you this a while ago, but it's always hard to know when."

And then they didn't say anything for a long time. I finished my lemon tart, chewed it to the last piece and swallowed it, and had a drink of water, and Mom said, "Well, Ellen, the new baby is coming—or rather, we are going to get her—in about a week."

"Where are you going to get her?"

"At the adoption agency in San Jose."

And, you know, for once in my life, I did not put two and two together. I just sat there. Finally, Dad said, "The same place where we had the good luck to get you, on the best day of our lives." He gave me a big smile, and Mom reached over and squeezed my hand. And then I put two and two together, and understood that I am adopted.

Chapter 5

I guess we talked about this for the next couple of hours, off and on. The main part of the story was that Mom and Dad really wanted a baby and tried really hard, but they could never have a baby. In the meantime, there are women, but they are girls, actually, something like sixteen years old or so, who do have babies, but they don't have the money to support them, and so they give them up for adoption, knowing that they will be loved and cared for in good homes. All of the information about where the baby came from and who ends up with the baby is secret forever—the new parents don't know who the mother and father were but they are very grateful for the mother being so generous to the baby and to them. The mother doesn't know where the baby went, and sometimes the baby can go a long way, but all of that is guessing, and it is better not to guess, but to look to the future, and know that the baby and the little girl and the new family will have a great life together.

Dad started talking about how this was a lot better than the old way, which was that lots of children lived in orphanages (I thought of his friend Jimmy Murphy, who he shot the beavers with, and maybe that was why he told me that story), but then Mom gave him a look, and he said we could talk about that another time. There are plenty of books about orphanages and orphans, though, and some of them are in my bookcase, so when I went up to my room after a while, I sat there and looked at them. Two of them are *Anne of Green Gables* and *Anne of Avonlea.* I read both of those around Christmas. There is also a cartoon in the paper called *Little Orphan Annie,* but I never read that, because Annie has no eyeballs, which is creepy. Snow White is an orphan and Cinderella is an orphan and Bambi is an orphan. The boy in a movie I saw, *The Sword in the Stone,* whose name was Wart, was an orphan. I watched that movie and read those books, and never once thought that I might be an orphan. But then, I am not an orphan. I have Mom and I have Dad, and I have this room and this house, and I can walk to Grandma Lydia and Grandpa John's anytime I want to, and all of them hug me and sometimes kiss me. I am not an orphan. I didn't take any of the orphan books off the shelf. I took down *The Bobbsey Twins at Home,* which I have read so many times that the back of the book broke off and had to be taped on again, and I started to read it. The last time I read it was last summer, when I was wishing that I had a twin or at least was not an only child, and here in a week, I will stop being an only child.

I was almost to the end of the second chapter when Mom came in to put me to bed. She smiled and didn't say anything about me being adopted; she just got some clean pajamas out of my drawer and turned back the quilt on my bed, then she stood there smiling while I cleaned my teeth, then she brushed my hair because if she doesn't, the tangles will be terrible in the morning, and it will be hard to get all the stuff done that we have to do before school. She knows that I know that she knows that I know that if I want to wear my hair long and not in braids or pigtails, the way I used to, I have to let her brush it twice a day, and so I do.

Once she'd tucked me in and turned on the night-light beside the door, she came back and sat on my bed. She said, "This has been a big day." Then she leaned down toward me and kissed me on the cheek, and she said in a soft voice, "After every big day, there is another day, and all the things that seemed big on that big day start getting smaller and smaller, until they are just regular things like everything else."

I said, "What are you going to name the baby?"

"We're going to name her Joan, which is a form of Johanna, after my aunt."

"What about her middle name?" My middle name is Rachel, which is just a name that my mom always liked.

"Ariel."

I had never heard of this name before, but I said, "That's a nice name. Joan Ariel Leinsdorf."

Looking at my mom there, with the starlight coming in the window, made me think two things—that I knew what a mom was and that I didn't know what a mom was—both at the same time. It was a funny feeling. She smoothed my hair back off my forehead and kissed me again, and then said, "I love you, Ellen. Go to sleep now."

After she left, I lay on my back, and that was when Ned started to talk to me for the first time. He was in the middle of the pasture, under some trees, all by himself. It was dark, and he was dark, too, so I couldn't see him very well. Then he turned his head, and I saw the little white strip and the glint of some sort of light on his shiny coat. He started pawing the ground, then he turned in a little circle, then he lay down and rolled, throwing his legs around and rubbing his back into the grass. After that, he stood up and shook himself, snorted, and said, "Do you have a pasture for me?"

I said, "I only have a garden. It is way too small for a horse."

"How big is it?"

"About the size of two stalls."

"I liked my stall at the racetrack. I don't really understand why I am here."

I said, "You hurt yourself in a race and they retired you."

"That is embarrassing."

"Do you remember hurting yourself?"

"I remember a hurt. There was a soft spot in the ground and I stepped right into it because the chestnut horse was pushing at me."

"He pushed you?"

"No. He pinned his ears and leaned toward me with his shoulder, and I leaned away from him and stepped in the hole."

I said, "Was he cheating?"

He said, "He knew what he was doing."

"Did the jockey know what the horse was doing?"

"Jockeys never know what we are doing."

That made me laugh.

Then he said, "These horses here think I'm a baby. They're always pinning their ears and picking up a back foot. That means 'Go away.'"

I said, "What about Gee Whiz?"

"Who's that?"

"The bigger gray."

"He's the worst. He thinks he is a stallion, he is so full of himself. He's always saying how he could jump out of the pasture, but he never does."

"Abby says he got out a couple of times, and also, he had dozens of starts."

"He already told me that."

"Abby likes you."

"She gives me a carrot sometimes. But all day long and all night long, I just stand around here. It's boring."

I said, "I know just what you mean."

And then he shook his head and ambled away. It was like he was walking away from the microphone or something. I had the sense that there was only one place in the pasture where he could talk to me. Until I fell asleep, I thought about his face and his short little forelock, and his shiny coat. I imagined doing what Abby does, which is to pet him from front to back, first the left side, and then the right side.

When I got home from school the next day, our house was already different. There was a bassinet in the guest room, and also a crib, for later, and on the mattress of the crib there was a stack of baby outfits, and another stack with diapers. Next to the crib was a diaper bucket (I know what this is—the diaper man drives up our street once a week, to pick up the dirty diapers and drop off the clean ones). Mom told me that Joan Ariel is already a week old—by the time we have her, she will be two weeks old. On the kitchen stove was a big pot, and inside it was a rack full of baby bottles. You sterilize them by boiling them for ten or fifteen minutes. After she put the roast in the oven, Mom took me into her room and sat me down on the bed, then she brought out a pink book and opened it.

It was my baby book, and there they were, pictures of Mom in a white hat and a light-colored jacket, and Dad in a shirt and tie, and Mom was smiling—she had me in her arms. I was very strange-looking—eyes closed and dark hair all over my head, bundled up in a blanket. First, they were standing in a doorway with some woman, and then they were walking down some steps, and then they were standing with Grandma and Grandpa in front of our house, and Mom was giving me a kiss on the forehead. I had never seen these photos before—the only baby picture I had seen was of when I was sitting in front of the Christmas tree. I don't know why I never asked why that was the only one. I said, "I hope Joan Ariel is cuter than I was," which made Mom laugh and kiss me, and she said, "Don't see how that could possibly happen."

On Wednesday, we had to give a report in reading class. I thought I was going to give a report about my riding lesson—that's what I always give reports about, unless I am assigned a book—but at the last minute, I stood up at the front of the room and said that I was getting a new sister in five days, that my mom and dad are adopting her, that she lives in San Jose, and that I am adopted, too, and then all these kids were staring at me, until Ruthie Creighton—whom I don't think I've ever talked to because she is as quiet as a mouse and always stays in the corner, and if she is going to go on the swings or climb the jungle gym, she only does it when she's by herself—said, "I'm adopted," and then everyone turned their heads and looked at her. Miss Cranfield said, "Thank you, Ellen, for your report." She smiled, first at me, then at Ruthie. Then she cleared her throat and said, "Let's see. All right, children. Marilyn Cooper, is your report ready?" Marilyn's report was about going to Disneyland. Her favorite ride was the Matterhorn. I happen to know that the Matterhorn is in Switzerland.

At lunchtime, I sat with my usual friends—Todd, who lives in a house that backs up to the Murphys', and Ann Aiello, who is in the other fourth-grade class, but was in my class in kindergarten, first, and second. We like to eat lunch together because she moved over the summer, and now her house is too far for me to walk to. The whole time we were eating lunch, I was looking at Ruthie Creighton. I mean, I knew she usually ate alone, and if she has a friend, I guess it is Linda Loring, who is very thin, and who my mom says has a hole in her heart, and so she can't go out for recess or do anything active. My mom says she is waiting for an operation. She is nice to Ruthie, but she doesn't come to school every day. Finally, Ann stopped talking about playing five-card stud with her cousins and winning three dollars and thirty-five cents, free and clear, and said, "Why are you looking at her?"

Since Ann isn't in my class, she didn't know about my report. So I said, "In our class, she said she was adopted."

Ann said, "She must be Catholic, then."

Now Todd put down his egg salad sandwich and said, "I'm Catholic."

We both looked at him. Ann said, "Duh. You go to my church."

Then he said, "My two cousins are adopted."

"See?" said Ann.

"They don't live around here, though. They live in Michigan."

I imagined two little babies being rescued from a frozen pile of snow and being laid in front of a big fire and brought back to life.

I said nothing about me being adopted. I figured Ann would learn soon enough and then she would tell Todd. Todd is in my class, and he would have heard me, but you have to tell him everything twice.

Chapter 6

On Thursday just before dinnertime, the phone rang. It was Abby. She said that Blue had an abscess in his foot, and could not be ridden this week, so would it be all right for me to come to the ranch again on Saturday? "I'll ride Sissy before you come, and I promise she will behave herself. In fact, if you want to, your dad can drop you off, and then you can have your lesson and stay for lunch, and we can bring you home, because my mom wants to go shopping at the department store where your mom works."

When you are talking about horses, an abscess is not such a bad thing. When they have one, they walk around as if they can't bear to put their foot down, but it goes away in a day or so. This happened with the pony. He looked like he had broken his ankle, but then two days later, this little tiny sore that's called a gravel appeared above the top edge of his hoof. The abscess happens when something gets inside the hoof. After that, he was fine, and everyone breathed a sigh of relief.

I asked her to hold on, then found Dad, who was taking a nap. He wasn't happy about making that long trip again, but believe me, I could read his mind—he was thinking, "Better give her what she wants for another few days, because after that, things will be really busy around here, and she might never get what she wants ever again." Well, maybe he wasn't thinking exactly that, but something like it, and so he said, "Sure." Abby said to be there at nine, which was fine with me, because I get up early anyway, Saturday, Sunday, every day.

That night, I tried to talk to Ned again, but he wouldn't do it. He just stood there in my head, not saying a thing. In the morning, I looked in the refrigerator for carrots and I found two. I broke them in pieces, took them up to my room, wrapped them in a washrag, and put them with my riding clothes so that I wouldn't forget them. In the meantime, more baby stuff kept appearing—a high chair, a baby carriage (this I recognized as a hand-me-down from the Murphys). When I said I had seen them pushing Brian in it, Mom said, "Honey, people are so generous when you are going to have a baby!" But our house is really small, so pretty soon everything was in the way, and there were two boxes, one of clothes and one of toys, that had to be stashed in my room.

Was I excited about the baby? When Mom asked me, I always said yes, but what I don't understand is how to be excited about someone you have never seen before. I knew enough about babies from walking around our neighborhood to understand that there would be crying and diaper rash and, in a year or two, running into the street. Ann has two sisters, but they are eleven and seven—she doesn't remember about babies. Todd is the youngest of six brothers. According to him, all his brothers talk about is cars and fishing. Even so, I did like saying her name, Joan Ariel, Joan Ariel, Joan Ariel. And I did imagine that someday she and I would be friends.

On Saturday, I had eaten my toast, which I made myself, and was dressed and ready to go by seven-thirty. Dad did get up in time, but he had to bring his second cup of coffee along. The good thing was that we were out early enough to miss *all* the traffic, and to get to Abby's by eight-thirty. She hadn't even been on a horse by the time we got there. She was still cleaning stalls, so I put my carrots in a place that I knew I would remember, and I helped her, which I don't mind doing—I think horse manure smells very nice, thank you. Most of Abby's horses stay outside, but two were staying in and the stalls are big. I was careful to use the fork to pick up the pieces of manure, and to shake the fork as I was lifting so that the straw would fall between the tines, because straw is expensive, and you want to save it. After I'd picked up the manure, I sifted through the straw and picked up the wet bunches. Horse pee is stinkier than manure, I think. Then we threw down some new bedding and tossed everything around with the forks so that the stall was all fluffed up and comfortable in case the horse wanted to lie down. Horses only sleep lying down a couple of hours a day, and some have their naps during the day, all stretched out in the straw or under a tree. By the time we were finished cleaning the stalls, Abby was laughing. She said that I should write a how-to book on cleaning stalls—all I would need to do is have someone take down everything

I say when I am doing it and talking about it at the same time. I said, "Abby, half the time I don't even realize that I am talking," and she laughed again.

When I go to the stables and ride Blue, I know that I'm supposed to help Rodney groom Blue and tack him up, and I do help him a little bit, but Rodney knows exactly what he's doing, and has been doing it for his whole life, because he started working as a groom in a steeplechase barn when he was thirteen years old, which was in 1933, the year a horse named Kellsboro Jack won the Grand National in record time, and also the year that a horse named Golden Miller won the Cheltenham Gold Cup for the second time out of five. The next year, Golden Miller won both the Cheltenham Gold Cup and the Grand National, the only horse ever to do that, and Rodney was at both races, because he worked for a trainer who had horses running. If I keep quiet and let Rodney tell me whatever he wants to about the old days in England, he does all the grooming and tacking up much more quickly and smoothly than I can. I just say, "Wow! Wow!" And I mean it, too. Rodney has seen a lot more races and places than just about anyone else, but he always tips his hat to everyone and says, "Thank ya, miss," as if you are the important one and he is not. So grooming Sissy and Gee Whiz (I had to help with that, too) was hard work, and then we walked to Abby's arena and I stood in the center, holding Gee Whiz while Abby worked Sissy.

I hadn't noticed on the way out to the ranch or in the barn, but the weather was cold and windy, almost as if winter were back. The hillside above the arena was scattered with poppies and lupine, and they were whipping around in the wind. The wind across the long green grass made wavy shapes against the hillside, and the branches of the trees were creaking, too. Sissy was not misbehaving, but she seemed much more wide-awake than she had the previous week, and Abby had her trot in a bunch of circles, as well as move from side to side at the walk and the trot, and step over behind in both directions. I can't say that Gee Whiz was bad, but he was alert. He looked up the hillside, and he looked back toward the pasture, and he looked out toward the road. One time, he tossed his head and pulled the reins out of my hand, but I said, "Hey!" and so he turned to look at me, and stood there quietly. He said, "Sorry. But there is a lot going on." He put his head down and I stroked him on the nose.

Right then, Ned and another horse galloped across the pasture, throwing their heads, bucking, and kicking. I would have thought that would excite Gee Whiz, but he just looked at them and turned away. He said, "Pip-squeaks."

I laughed, then I said, "You should be nicer to Ned. He doesn't like you."

Gee Whiz didn't say anything. He lifted his head and looked over me at Abby and Sissy. After fifteen minutes of work (I looked at my watch), Abby walked Sissy to us and dismounted. She said, "She seems fairly relaxed. I think she'll give you a good ride, but it's too windy to go on the trail."

I led Sissy to the railing, sided her up, and climbed the fence. As soon as I was ready to get on, she moved away, so I climbed down, put her back in position, and climbed the fence again. This time, she pivoted her hind end away from me. And she was looking me right in the eye. She didn't say anything, but her look said, "I have had enough." I put my hands on my hips. Abby came over to help me, leading Gee Whiz, and as soon as Sissy saw them heading our way, she pivoted back into position, and waited while I sort of jumped onto her.

I sat up straight, lowered my heels, turned my thumbs up, loosened my elbows, and made my butt as heavy as I could. No one tells you to do this, but that's what they mean when they say "Sit deep." I gave Sissy a good kick, out, in, and she walked forward. The first two steps were balky, like the week before, but then she must have decided that she had better get her work done, and so she stepped out, started swinging back and forth a little, and did what I told her to do. Since she doesn't jump, we practiced all those boring things that you have to practice when you aren't jumping.

Except that since Sissy had decided to do her job, and maybe to enjoy it, riding her was fun. She had a nice, loose walk. I held the reins as lightly as I could, and her hips seemed to swing back and forth. I could feel each hind leg stepping through, which means that with each step, the horse puts her hind foot down in front of where the front foot had been. When a horse does that, even the walk is fun and not lazy. The horse seems to be going where she wants to go, but not to be rushing there. Abby had me do a movement she calls the snake dance—lots of S-turns back and forth, back and forth, down the long side of the arena—asking

Sissy to bend her body first to the left and then to the right, with always an absolutely straight step in between. It is pretty easy to do at the walk, harder at the trot. I can't do it at the canter, because it involves a series of flying changes, but I have seen Abby do it on Blue, and it is very beautiful to watch, and always makes Abby grin when she is doing it. After the snake dance at the trot, we did the bow: you walk down the long side to the end of the arena, loop around, walk back to the center of the long side, go the other way, loop again, walk back, then do it at the trot. Sissy seemed to like this exercise. The next level, which Abby showed me on Gee Whiz, includes something called a leg-yield, which Abby learned about in a book she's reading. After the horse loops around, he stays pointed forward as if he were going to go straight, but steps to the side so that his back legs cross each other. Gee Whiz was quite good at this. Another thing we did was a weaving exercise, where I would trot in front of Abby and pass her, then she would trot in front of me and pass me, back and forth. This was sort of hard to do, because Gee Whiz has a much bigger trot than Sissy, but Abby said that it was good for them to pay attention and rate themselves. For the canter, we played follow-the-leader—first Abby leading, and then me. We had to go around in circles large and small, change leads, go faster or slower, but never stop cantering. Sissy turned out to have a nice canter, so that was the most fun part. I have to admit that I enjoyed myself so much that I stopped watching Ned, or waiting for him to say something to me, and I made up my mind that one of the carrots had to be for Sissy.

By the time we had the horses cooled out and un-tacked, the wind had blown the clouds in and it looked like it might rain, which was a disappointment, because where I live it rains a lot more than where Abby lives, so I always expect sunshine when I go out there. We put Sissy in with the other mares and Gee Whiz in with the other geldings, and then Abby said, "Come here," and we went into the gelding pasture and stood quietly. Ned and the other horse, a buckskin, were grazing over in the corner, maybe ten feet from each other, not like they were friends, but like they were getting used to each other. I said, "Where is the buck-ing bronco?" This was a horse who lived here over the winter. His owner was a friend of Abby's brother.

"He's on the circuit, doing his job."

"Doesn't all that bucking hurt those horses?"

"Not if they don't get jolted or prodded. If they just buck for the love of bucking, like Beebop, they can last a long time. I've never seen Beebop at a rodeo in person, but in his pictures, his face is relaxed even when his back hooves are practically over his head and the cowboy is flying through the air. Anyway, I don't know what they would do with him if he didn't go to rodeos. He can't be ridden."

I said, "They should teach him tricks."

Abby looked at me. Out of the corner of my eye, I could see Ned heading our way, but not quickly. I had the carrots in my pocket, but my hands were empty. Abby glanced in his direction, too, then said, "Let's think of a trick. Close your eyes."

I closed my eyes.

It wasn't hard to think of a trick, because while we were riding, Abby's dog, Rusty, a big wolfy type of dog, had trotted by the arena with a stick in her mouth, not as if she was fetching, but as if she had a project. If I were to have another dog, I would want one like her. I opened my eyes and said, "Fetching. I would teach the horse to fetch something like a hat. Like my dad's hat. What about you?"

Abby said, "Finding something is fun. I taught Blue

to look at a treat and then find it. He got to be very careful with his lips. I could put a cube of sugar on the top of a fence post, and he could find it without knocking it off."

Ned bumped into me from behind, just very gently. I hadn't realized that he was so close. Abby looked at me and said, "Turn around and tell him to back. He shouldn't get that close to you. Put your hand up, with your palm facing him, and tell him." So I turned slowly around, lifted my hand, and said, "Ned, back!" We waited. Ned flicked his ears and said, "What in the world are you talking about?"

I laughed.

Abby said, "Why are you laughing?" I knew not to tell her that Ned was talking to me, so I said, "Oh, he just has a funny face."

"He does," said Abby.

He stood there for a long moment. I could tell that he was sniffing my pocket. Finally, Abby said, "I guess he needs a lesson." She was still carrying the halter, so she put it on Ned. But she didn't tell him to back, or back him up. Instead, she turned his head to the right and held it like that until he stepped his right back leg across his left one and moved his hind end to the side. Then she did it again on that side, and twice on the other side. Ned was saying, "What is it that I am supposed to do here?" I didn't answer because I didn't want Abby to think I was crazy. She did it on both sides again, and by now he seemed to understand *what* he was supposed to do, if not why. She said, "There he goes. He's getting it." I said, "Tell me again why you do that?"

"To make him soft and relaxed in his spine. Everything is easier if he is relaxed. See? He's taking a deep breath."

And he was.

Now she stepped in front of him, about two steps out, and after standing quietly for a moment, she shook the lead rope under his chin and said, "Back! Ned, back!" He tossed his head, leaned backward, and then stepped about half a step back. Now she petted him, praised him, and put her hand in her pocket. Then she said, "Oh darn! I don't have anything! Do you? Give him something—quick!" So I pulled my hand out of my pocket and gave him one of the carrot pieces. Then we petted him.

She said, "He knows nothing."

He said, "That's not true!"

I felt like I do when my mom and dad are having an argument. They never raise their voices, but I know they're upset, and I'm stuck in the middle. Finally, I said, "He reminds me of a puppy. He's so—" And right then, Ned snorted. I hadn't thought I was being insulting, but as Miss Cranfield was always telling me, "Ellen, you need to think before you speak."

Ned said, "Puppy!" and Gee Whiz, who was still over by the gate, eating some grass, lifted his head and looked at us and said, "Yup."

I looked at Abby and said, "I meant that to be nice." But I was talking to the horses. "Everybody loves puppies."

Ned snorted again.

Abby got him to back up three more times, each time for a piece of carrot, and then when she was done, I petted him and gave him a whole carrot. We walked away, and I wondered if Ned would ever talk to me again. When we came back a half hour later to put out their noon hay, Ned was way over on the far side of the pasture. There was plenty of grass, since it is spring, so even when he saw the hay, he just looked at it and went back to grazing.

Chapter 7

Even though Abby is older than I am, and her brother is old enough to be in the army, her mom is really young-looking and hardly looks like a mom at all. She smiles as if she means it, and she doesn't seem as though she's always watching you to see if you are doing something wrong. Her dad is a little scary, though. He is really tall and looks like he is strong enough to throw a hay bale overhand, like a football. His eyebrows kind of lower down over his eyes. Everyone at the stables says that he is a wizard with horses. Nobody thinks I know much, but I keep my ears open even while I am talking, and I know that Melinda's mom got lots of money for the pony. Before the pony, Abby sold Black George to Sophia for a lot of money, and Rodney says that people offer Sophia just about anything she would ask to buy him, but Sophia says that jumping a course on Black George, whom she calls Onyx, is a form of relaxation, and if she didn't have him, then she couldn't ride Pie in the Sky at all—she needs both of them—and when I think of her saying this, I think of the time she fell off like she was doing a cartwheel, and I believe her. Blue's owner died a week after bringing him to the stables, and Jane sold him to Abby for a dollar or something like that, which was the amount of money she had in her pocket at the time. (Later, Abby sold him to the stable for a lot more than a dollar.) I'm sure that Mr. Lovitt was fit to be tied, as Grandma Lydia would say. Anyway, Mr. Lovitt goes every year to Oklahoma, where they once lived, and buys horses there and brings them to California. Jane told my mom that he sees something in them that no one else does, and it is a rare talent. I think all of these things as I am sitting at the table, eating my chili, which is what we have for lunch, along with corn bread and some fresh lettuce from Abby's mom's garden. I know Mr. Lovitt is not trying to scare me, but I jump anyway when he says, "So, Ellen, what do you think of Sissy?"

And as soon as that booms out, I stop talking and can't even remember what I think of Sissy. I can feel my mouth drop open, and I make myself close it. Abby says, "Sissy worked hard today."

He says, "That's a change."

I say, "I like Sissy." I sound like I am whispering. So I clear my throat and say, "Sissy has a future."

He laughs and says, "I should hope so. She's only six." His voice is loud. Abby and her mother don't seem to notice.

That makes me blush, as if I said a stupid thing. It is really funny the way you are not the same person for everyone. I think that if Miss Cranfield were a fly on the wall and saw how shy and quiet I am around Mr. Lovitt, she wouldn't believe her own eyes.

After lunch, I had to wait while Abby rode Oh My, a very pretty paint. Sometimes the Lovitts have cattle around, but they didn't have any around this spring. I knew I was going to have to wait, so I brought my book with me—*Misty of Chincoteague,* which I've already read four times. I got it out of the barn, where I had put it with my sweater (now I would probably forget my sweater), and carried it over to the back porch and opened it to chapter three. I read a page. But from Abby's back porch, you can see the geldings in their pasture, and so of course I started watching Ned, but I didn't try to talk to him.

Abby's dad was on one of the mares, and Rusty was following him. They were at the top of the hill behind the pasture, walking slowly along the fence. At every post, the horse would stop, and Abby's dad would reach over and jiggle the post, then walk on. Ned was watching them, his ears pricked. One time, he whinnied, and then one of the mares in the mare pasture whinnied, but the horse Abby's dad was on didn't pay any attention. I thought all of a sudden of Ruthie Creighton, the way she would look at the other kids sometimes at lunch. She is a strange girl. We all wear kneesocks, and kneesocks always slide down your leg and you have to pull them up, but Ruthie sometimes lets hers go all the way down and bunch in her shoes. Lots of times you can tell that no one brushes her hair—she just pushes it out of her face, and there are plenty of tangles. Her clothes are nice enough, mostly like the clothes that all the other girls wear, but they are wrinkled, and sometimes she buttons the buttons wrong and doesn't notice. As I was thinking this, it came to me that maybe she needs a trainer, just like a horse. Maybe if she is an only child, there is no one to tell her or show her things. I don't know where her house is, but it can't be too far from my house. I started to wonder if I should walk over there, just walk down the street, and have a look. I imagined Ruthie coming out the front door looking like all the other kids, and then letting everything go, step by step, on the way to school. This is a problem with being an only child—most of the time it's your brothers and sisters who tell you what to do, especially when, as Mrs. Murphy says, "I can't be everywhere at once!" I am lucky that I have not only Mom and Dad, but also Grandpa and Grandma. But clearly, Ruthie isn't lucky.

I set down my book and walked along the fence of the gelding pasture until I was pretty close to Ned. I climbed onto the fence and sat there. Ned looked at me (I have given him some treats, after all), and I said, "Okay, Ned. Tell me what you know."

"I know how to break from the gate. If you have an outside post, you have to break fast and cross to the railing right away, or the other horses will block you. If you have an inside post, you can jump out and go to the front, but then you have to run fast all the way.

You can also break slow and hold back, then when the others run out of steam, you can get through and into the lead."

"Did you ever win?"

"No, but I saw how it was done. I might have. I was fifth once, fourth once, and then third."

"Why didn't you win?"

"I don't know."

"Pip-squeak," said Gee Whiz as he walked by.

Ned pinned his ears.

I said, "What else do you know?"

He said, "I know to switch leads on the turn. When you break from the gate, you are on the outside lead, but that will slow you down on the turn. The horses who can't switch leads get very tired."

"Did you think racing was tiring?"

"No. This is tiring. Having nothing to do."

I thought of Ruthie again, and said, "Who were your friends there?"

He said, "I liked my morning rider. He was nice to me. He didn't hold me tight and he had good balance. If I got nervous, he would sing me a song."

"What was his name?"

"Alfredo."

"Who else?"

He curled his lip and blew out some air. I took this to mean that he didn't have any other friends at the track. I said, "What about other horses?"

"Other horses aren't your friends."

"Ever?"

"Never."

By now, Ned was standing near me, and finally, he came over and nudged me with his nose. Abby would have said that he wanted a treat and that he should have to earn one, but I was thinking of Ruthie. I decided that he wanted some petting, so that is what I gave him—smooth, easy strokes on his cheek and under his mane. He seemed to like it, because he put his head down and let me do it. Gee Whiz was looking at us, but didn't say anything.

By the time we left Abby's ranch in the car, it was really cloudy, and as we got closer to where I live, it started to rain. Abby and her mom were smiling. Her mom said, "I always love a late rain. The hills stay green longer. I hope we get at least half an inch."

Abby nodded. They were both different from the

way they are at the ranch or at the stables—it was like they were on a vacation. Abby's mom said, "So, Ellen, is your mom still working Fridays and Saturdays? I hope she can help me find something nice. Bright."

Abby lifted her eyebrows.

Her mom said, "But not too bright."

I said, "She's working this week. But Monday we get the baby, so she might not go back." This was the first time I had thought of this part of it.

"What baby?" said Abby.

"Joan Ariel, our new baby. We're going up to San Jose to get her Monday." I pretended this was the way you always got babies, but in fact, I wasn't quite sure about how you got babies. I hadn't ever thought about it before, and when the Murphys came home with Brian, my dad said, "Where in the world did they get yet another one?" And then my mom said, "Your aunt was one of thirteen, and her cousin was one of ten."

And Dad said, "Those days are long gone. Someone should tell the Murphys." That was four years ago, and people don't think I can remember that far back, but I can.

We drove without talking, just listening to the rain on the roof of the car and the swish of the windshield wipers, and then I said, "I'm adopted, too. Mom and Dad told me last week."

"I didn't know that," said Abby.

"Well," said her mom. "It's no one else's business, really."

I said, "Why?"

She said, "All those are private things. Every family has secrets that they keep to themselves."

I said, "Like what?" It is really true that I was just curious here. I wasn't asking for a secret, but there was a long silence, and then I said I was sorry, but I wasn't quite sure what I was sorry about. When we turned down the hill toward my house, where they were going to drop me off, I decided that I was sorry I had told my family's secret. When Abby's mom pulled over and stopped in front of the house, Abby said, "I'm sure Blue will be fine by next week, but I will let you know. And you did a good job on Sissy."

"I liked her." Then I remembered my manners, and said, "Thank you for lunch, Mrs. Lovitt."

"Ellen, you can come anytime. It's nice to have you."

She leaned out the window of the car and squeezed my hand and smiled. They drove away. It was a little cold, and I realized that I had forgotten my sweater.

Mom was at work and Dad was reading some papers. Even in the few hours that I'd been gone, more stuff had come into the house, and because it is a small house, now the whole place looked like a nursery—baby clothes stacked on the couch, baby swing in the living room, high chair back in the corner of the kitchen. I babbled on about my riding lesson and how great I had been, but I was hardly even listening to myself, I was so busy looking at all the new stuff. Dad nodded and nodded and then said, "I'm sure you were terrific, Ellen." He didn't seem very happy, but that wasn't my business.

Chapter 8

When I looked out my window before going to bed, the sky was clear and there was a quarter of a moon. Usually that meant that the sky was also clear at Abby's ranch, and this time when I closed my eyes, I saw Ned better than the last time. He was standing in a spot in the back of the pasture near the fence line, down from where Abby's dad had been riding that afternoon. The moon sat on top of the hill like a little bowl, just about to go down, but still bright. There were also plenty of stars. I saw the Big Dipper and Orion. Dad likes stars and tells me their names when we walk down by the ocean sometimes. The other horses weren't around— maybe off to the side, under a tree, a pale mound that was Gee Whiz was taking a nice nap. It was very quiet.

In our town, cars go up and down the street, and past my school, pretty much all night long, but where Abby lives, the only things you hear are birds and coyotes and the sound of the wind making the trees creak.

Ned said, "It takes a long time to make a friend."

I said, "Why is that?"

I didn't think he was going to answer, and I started to fall asleep—it had been a long day, and it was very late. But then he said, "On the farm, before we went into training, we ran around in a big pasture with lots of grass. Much bigger than this one, and trees only along the fence, not in the pasture. We ran and ran and ran. We kicked up and we bucked and we played. The other yearlings would do a lot of things. One time, one of them found something draped over the fence. We didn't even know what it was. He grabbed it and ran with it, and tossed it into the air. Some others tried to grab it from him. That was fun. I later realized that it was a saddle pad someone had left on the fence."

I made myself wake up and pay attention.

"At night, we lay down in the grass and rested or slept. I had a friend then, a yearling who looked like me, but had a white foot and a big blaze. We slept near each other, and raced each other. We were evenly matched. Sometimes he won and sometimes I won. He was my friend."

I said, "What was his name?"

"He didn't have a name."

"Did you have a name?"

"No. Not until I went into training. We got sold at the same auction. I never saw him after that. When I was at the racetrack, it was so big, and there were so many horses, that I thought he might turn up, so when I went out to train in the mornings, I would look for him, but I never saw him. That was my friend."

I didn't say anything. I thought this was a sad story, and anyway, it sounded like school, didn't it? Lots of kids thrown together in a big group, and you make what you can out of the kids in your class. Ann tells me every day at lunch that she hasn't really found a friend in her class—at least, as good a friend as I am. But when our class walked down the hall and passed her classroom Friday, the door was open, and I could see her in there, laughing with Audrey Snediger like they were friends. And I joke around with Jimmy Murphy and some of the other kids, even though I always sit with Ann and Todd. Is Todd my friend? I spend time with him. Is Abby my friend? She's my teacher, and she treats me as if she likes me. Is Rodney my friend? I love his stories and he's always nice to me. There are three girls in my class—Jane Ann Carroll, Martha King, and Carla Pinkerton—who always talk about how they are best friends and have been all their lives (they live on the same street) and will always be best friends until forever. But anyone can see that they have lots of fights and stop talking to one another for days until they make up and have a slumber party or something. The story Ned told me made me wonder just exactly what a friend is.

I was tired. I think we could have talked about more things, but my eyes just closed, and the next thing I knew, it was morning, and the sun was bright in my window, because I slept until eight. The house was really quiet, but when I got up and looked out, I saw that Mom was in the garden, planting something. The mower was out, too, so I guess she was going to mow the grass in the garden one last time. The patch of grass is about as big as the rug in our living room, but it is thick and green, and Mom is proud of it. I put on my clothes and went down for breakfast—waffles and sausage links. I could see that the spoiling was going to continue, and that was fine with me.

I was eating my second waffle when Mom came in from the garden. I said, "Did Abby's mom buy a nice dress?"

"I liked it. It was on sale, marked down from last spring, but it looked very nice on her, and she doesn't care about style. We're facing the hem and taking it down two inches. She would never wear a miniskirt, for sure."

I said, "She would look good in a miniskirt."

"Well, he wouldn't allow *that*."

I knew she was talking about Abby's dad. I said, "He's a little scary."

She tossed her hand. "Opinionated. He means well. I guess the boy, what's-his-name, Dan, is off to North Carolina for some sort of training. That's a ways. But she says he's just as happy to be seeing the world as to be sticking around here all his life. That's the way your dad was. But he wanted to go west, not east."

I said, "What about you?"

"Right here is fine with me. Right here, with you and your dad and your new sister. That is my idea of heaven on earth." And she came over and kissed me on the forehead and gave me a little squeeze around the shoulders.

All day long, we just did the things we wanted to do, and in the afternoon one of the things I wanted to do was go for a little walk, which I did. Mom went along, but I led the way. I walked around the school, looking down every block, and at the houses, and I paid attention to the street names. I hadn't figured out how to get Ruthie to tell me her address, but when she did, I wanted to be able to see her house in my mind. On our way home, Mrs. Murphy stopped us. She was standing on her front porch, clanging her bell. She said that Jimmy and Luke, who is a year older than Jimmy, had gone down to the beach to look for starfish. If the wind was right, they could hear the bell; otherwise, she had to send one of the girls after them. But she ran down to the street and gave Mom a big hug, and said, "Louise, I am so happy for you! I will be the first to pay a visit, whenever you want, and I have about two hours' worth of advice, so don't dare ask me, or I will talk your ear off." Mom laughed, and as we walked home, I said, "Is the adoption supposed to be a secret?"

"Nothing is a secret in this town, and anyway, even if you wanted it to be a secret, there you are, one day, pushing a baby carriage around town."

"Abby's mom thought it was a secret."

Mom was quiet for a moment, then said, "When you live out in the middle of nowhere, you think you have secrets maybe even when you don't."

This made me think about secrets until I went to sleep. I have no secrets because I talk all the time. I'm not sure whether that is good or bad.

The first surprise about Joan Ariel was that when I wasn't dressed for school at seven-thirty on Monday, Mom said, "What is going on?"

I said, "We're going to get the baby." Then I said, "Joan Ariel," just to be helpful. Mom laughed and said, "Oh! *That* baby!" but then she shook her head, leaned toward me, and said, "You have to go to school, and then your grandma will be here when you get home. Your dad and I are going to get the baby."

There are a lot of places where kids aren't allowed, and I decided that the orphanage must be one of them. I imagined it as sort of like a big pet store, where the puppies are in little pens, and all the things you need for the puppy are right nearby, on shelves. Maybe Mom had been there before, and walked around and chosen Joan Ariel because she was the cutest or the only girl. I have been in a lot of pet stores, and I always like the puppy that looks right at you, wagging his tail and jumping up and down, ready to play. I thought about this as I was putting on my clothes. And then I didn't think about anything, because I was almost late for school, and I was the last person to sit in my chair before the bell rang.

At lunch, I must have talked on and on about Joan Ariel (*not* a secret), because Ann and Todd didn't say anything, and every so often nodded and smiled, and then Todd ran off to play with the boys, and Ann and I went out for after-lunch recess. Instead of sticking with me, she went to some girls in her class, and even though they weren't mean to me or anything, I felt a little like Ned in the pasture, not very important. But what did I care? I couldn't stop thinking about Joan Ariel, but I did shut up.

One thing all my report cards say about me is that I am always busy, and if only I wouldn't get distracted, I would do better in school. It is true that I'm always busy, but I don't get distracted. I just like to do what I want to do, and only sometimes is that the same thing that the teacher wants me to do. Miss Cranfield is really good about this. If I have done my work for school, then she ignores me when I am doing other things, so in the last week, I had made eleven drawings of Ned's head. After

I finished my multiplication problems, I opened the lid of my desk and looked at them. Of course, I put the day I drew each one on the lower right-hand corner, because it is better to be organized. I closed my eyes and pictured Ned in my mind. The problem was that now that I had seen him more, I wasn't so sure what he looked like, and I thought that all the pictures were wrong. Sometimes an ear was right and sometimes an eye. The line of his face is straight, so it is easy to get that right. Miss Cranfield said, "Ellen!" She was standing right beside me. I jumped and banged my head on the lid of the desk, and then it dropped and landed on my hand and I said, "Dammit." About six or seven kids laughed out loud, and Miss Cranfield gave me a dirty look, and then she pointed to my multiplication sheet, which had fallen to the floor and now had a footprint on it—my footprint. I bent down and picked it up. She took it between her thumb and forefinger and said, "Ellen, why don't you take a break."

This meant that I had to go out and sit in the hall. It wasn't me who was taking the break, it was her.

I passed Ruthie Creighton on the way out. She was staring up at me with her mouth open. I also passed Todd, who smiled but then hiccuped.

I don't mind sitting in the hall. I've only done it a couple of times. It's quiet and cool—there isn't any sunshine in the hall. Sometimes I make up a story. This time, I imagined Mom and Dad leaving the house all dressed up, and getting into the car. Then I thought about them driving past the school, up the hill, turning onto the highway, and heading to San Jose, out into the sun, past the fields and the mountains in the distance. The windows are down because it is hot, and Mom is holding her hat on, trying to keep her hair out of her face. Dad says, "Joan Ariel will be a wonderful child," and Mom says, "But not better than Ellen." Then they both nod.

Miss Cranfield opened the door after a while and said, "Ten minutes are up. You can come back in, Ellen, but I want you to stay after school so that I can talk to you about a few things."

I said, "Am I in trouble?"

She said, "Not exactly."

I have to say that I always think it is better if they say "yes" or "no." It's like they do not know what they mean. I always know what I mean.

Chapter 9

All the other kids picked up their lunch boxes and their sweaters and walked out of the room. I stayed sitting at my desk. Miss Cranfield put some things in drawers, then got up and put the chalk and the erasers at one end of the blackboard. At last, she looked at me and made a little wave with her hand, so I went and stood in front of her desk.

She said, "The first thing I want you to know, Ellen, is that you aren't in trouble."

I said, "I know that."

She acted like she didn't hear me, and went on, "Sometimes when things get to be just too much, people have to take a break."

I said, "I didn't mind taking a break."

She sighed and said, "Good. Good. I told the class that you weren't in trouble."

I said, "I hope they believed you."

"Well, perhaps they did. Anyway, your mom told Mr. Gretzky what she and your dad are doing today, and he told me. Sometimes big changes can be a little overwhelming, and when they are, children get a little disorganized. . . ." Mr. Gretzky is our principal.

"I wasn't disorganized. I was organized. I was looking at my horse pictures, and deciding if any of them were good. I was finished with my problems."

"I saw that you drew a couple of horse pictures on the back of one of your papers."

"Did you like them?"

"Well, that isn't really the place for them."

"That was why I drew them on the back. Did you like them?"

"Ellen, I don't think it's a good idea to encourage you."

"Why not?" I was not trying to be sassy. I really wondered.

Miss Cranfield looked me right in the eye, and the look on her face said two things. One of them was "I don't know" and the other one was "I am losing my patience here." It's really hard to make Miss Cranfield lose her patience. She's been teaching in our school since my mom was in fifth grade. My mom never had her, because Miss Cranfield started with the first graders, but when we have Open School Night, my mom and Miss Cranfield always give each other a little kiss on the cheek and seem happy to see each other. She doesn't live in our town, but down the coast.

Finally, she sat back in her chair, stacked her papers together, and gave her biggest sigh. At last, she said, "What I would really like you to do for the rest of the school year, which is only about six weeks at this point, is to practice paying attention and following instructions. You have a lot of practice doing things the way you want to, but very little practice doing things the way you're supposed to." She leaned forward. "In order to do well, you have to know how to do it both ways— your way, and someone else's way—and to know when each way is appropriate. Do you hear me?"

I nodded.

"Okay, you can go."

I went.

Grandma Lydia was standing on the front porch waiting for me when I got to the house. She said, "Good heavens! It's nearly three-thirty!"

I told her that I had to stay after school, even though I wasn't in trouble, and she clucked and shook her head and said, "They could at least call!" but she didn't sound angry, and I have often heard Mom say, "Why in the world is she such a worrier!" She held the door open for me, and we went into the house. Of course, there was a whole plate full of oatmeal cookies on the kitchen table, still warm, and the kitchen smelled wonderful. Grandma Lydia always says that if she has a minute, she would just like to make something, and so she does, and my favorite thing she makes is the oatmeal cookies, and so the spoiling was continuing. We sat across the table from one another, and she smiled while I ate my cookie and drank a glass of milk.

After I had eaten the last crumb, I said, "Do you remember the day Mom and Dad brought me home from the orphanage?"

"You mean the agency, but of course I do. It was only nine years ago, sweetheart. That's no time to an old lady."

I said, "How old are you?"

She laughed. "I'm sixty-five, but don't you dare tell anyone."

"So what was it like?"

"Oh, goodness, well, it was foggy, for one thing. That was a foggy summer, it kept coming and going. Your mom so wanted to have a nice day for you, but we could barely see our hands in front of our faces. So, let's see. You were seven weeks old—"

"Joan Ariel is two weeks old."

"Oh, goodness, I knew a child, didn't get out of the home until she was over a year. She was walking and everything! You hope for the best, but you never can predict. Anyway, you were already smiling—that's the first thing I remember. Your mom kind of leaned over you and had you covered so your face wouldn't get damp, and then she came in the house here, and folded back the blanket, and you had such a big smile on your face. Ear to ear. And such thick hair. Just black. That all fell out. Always does. And then it came in like it is now, more brown and shiny. I knew one other baby who was like that—born with thick blond hair, just white-blond, that fell out and came in red."

"Was I a good baby?"

"Oh, heavens me. Well, you meant to be good, but

you were very opinionated. Every time we offered you something, you stared at it as if you had to make up your own mind. You walked at a year. I woke up at night worrying about the stairs, but you taught yourself to go down them, up and down, all day long. It was good exercise. I remember one time your mom had you at the department store, and I guess she bent down to look closely at some dress she was interested in, and when she stood up, you were holding on to the skirt of the dress you liked. It was red." She put her head back and laughed, then looked at me. "When I was your age, we were told to sit quietly and speak only when spoken to. Isn't that ridiculous? But that was the way back then. When your grandpa was in school, they would paddle him, and cane him on the hand. He had to hold out his hand, and the teacher would smack it with some kind of flexible cane, make it so it hurt as much as possible. I swear, were people that much stupider back then? Seems to me like they were."

Now she looked at me. "Well, I guess get out of your school clothes, into something comfortable. We might have a long wait, might not." She stood up and picked up my dirty glass. I went upstairs. There was nothing new in my room, at least. I went to my window and opened it, and all the fragrances of all the flowers planted around the yard came blowing in. I hadn't said that I would be good all the time for the next six weeks. I had only said that I heard what Miss Cranfield was saying, so I would not be breaking any promises by not being good. I knew that, even if she did not. But I also had this little feeling, like we were close to some edge—all of us: Mom and Dad because of Joan Ariel, and Grandma because she was baking so many cookies and remembering when she was young, and Miss Cranfield because the end of the year was coming, which in my experience always makes teachers nervous, and maybe that is because some kids have to be flunked and some kids have to be sent to the principal's office. Which is not to say that edges are all bad. You can get to the edge of the high dive at the swimming pool and then jump off and it feels wonderful and you want to do it again and again. But it still feels like an edge.

A voice said, "Knock knock!" and I said, "Who's there?" and the voice said, "Ned!"

Mostly, I talked to Ned at night, when I was lying in

the dark. I had to be lying on my back, too, and kind of looking at the ceiling. Now I laughed to myself, leaned my elbows on the windowsill, and closed my eyes.

He said, "He's here."

I said, "Who's there?"

"My friend."

"Your friend from a long time ago?"

"Yes. We knew each other as soon as he stepped off the trailer. He whinnied. I couldn't see him, but I heard him. I knew it was him, and then they walked him around the house and along the fence, and I whinnied, and he looked at me. They call him Ben."

"Ben and Ned?"

"That's who we are, at least here."

"Does he still look like you?"

"He's bigger, a little longer in the leg. Maybe humans wouldn't think we look alike, but to us we do."

I opened my eyes and thought for a while about whether I should ask my next question. There were two little birds across the way, building their nest in one of the trees. I watched them for a moment, then said, "Is he nice to you?"

"We touched noses and sniffed each other. We played a little. He's standing right here."

But I didn't see him. I said, "Will he talk to me?"

"No. He doesn't know how."

I said, "What has he been doing?"

"He never went to the track. He hurt himself at the training farm, then was out for a year."

I said, "What does Gee Whiz have to say?"

"He just kicked up and walked away."

Just then, I heard a car in the driveway, and I knew that Mom and Dad and Joan Ariel had arrived, and I have to say that Ned went right out of my head at that very moment. I didn't even change my clothes, the way Grandma had told me to. I went out in the hall. I thought I was going to run down the stairs, but then the front door opened—I could see it from the landing—and all of a sudden, I felt afraid, though I have no idea what I was afraid of. I stood there with my hand on the banister. Dad must have been holding the door open—he does that—and here came Mom, and she had a bundle in her arms wrapped in pink blankets. Dad came in right after her, and Grandma was there, saying, "Oh my, look at that!" and when everyone got quiet, I could hear this little sound, not crying, but this meeping, cheeping sound. Mom looked up the stairs and said, "Sweetie, come down!" And so

I went down, step by step. I watched my feet, which I haven't had to do since I was five years old and learning to go down the right way rather than one foot at a time. It was like that edge I had been thinking about. Here it was. Joan Ariel suddenly seemed very scary. My heart was pounding, too. I could feel it. I decided that I would be a good girl, maybe not for six whole weeks, but at least for now.

When I got to the bottom of the stairs, Dad took my hand and gave me a kiss and then Mom leaned down and there was Joan Ariel, all wrapped up, only her face showing, and I have to admit that I had never seen anything like her in my whole life, so tiny and reddish and with her eyes kind of crossed, not like any picture of a baby, or any baby in the movies or on TV that you ever saw, and it did occur to me that maybe we got her because no one else wanted her, but I didn't say it— even I knew better than to say that—and I kissed her on the cheek, and Mom said, "Just don't kiss her on the lips," but I wouldn't have done that anyway.

Mom carried her over to the couch, sat down, and laid Joan Ariel down beside her and opened up the blanket. Mom was smiling like it was Christmas. The meeping and cheeping got louder when the blanket was opened, and in the meantime, Grandma went into the kitchen and returned with a baby bottle. She gave it to Mom, then settled back on her heels with her hands on her hips, also smiling like mad, and I guess that's when my new life began.

Chapter 10

Apparently, it takes two people to take care of a baby, because Grandma Lydia stayed that evening and made supper. Grandpa came over, too, to have a look at Joan Ariel. The next morning, Grandma showed up before I even came down for breakfast—and she made me pancakes. Dad was already gone on his vacuum-cleaner trip for the week—he had to rush down to Los Angeles, which is a long drive, and then get in lots of showings, because Mom did in fact quit her job at the department store, at least for the time being. Grandma kissed me way before I left for school, and went upstairs, and I got myself dressed and out the door, and it is certainly a good thing that I wear a watch and know what time it is. There are kids in my class who still can't tell time, if you can believe it, or at least they pretend that they can't. We had stewed tomatoes at lunch, and a bunch of sixth graders sang a song: "Stewed tomatoes, together we've hated you! Of course, that is nothing new—we hate cabbage, too. All hate! All hate! The tomatoes that Johnny ate!" Johnny must have been Johnny Cain, because he then stood up at the end of his table, and pretended to throw up on his plate, and everyone laughed, and Mr. Nelson, the sixth-grade teacher, walked him out of the lunchroom.

By the end of the day, I felt like I had been at school for my whole life, even though I knew this wasn't true.

And maybe the fact that I was now supposed to pay attention in class every minute and do everything that I was told to do was part of the problem, because I knew that Miss Cranfield was watching me, so I didn't even look at the alphabet or keep track of saying it backward to myself, nor did I look out the window, nor did I say anything to Ned, nor did I draw a horse or even a tic-tac-toe on my paper. One thing I did do was erase a bunch of answers to questions on the spelling test, and then on the multiplication paper, and write them in again more neatly—not because the answers were wrong but because I was so bored—and then I looked over at this girl in our class who is always number one, Kathleen Kernan. I know that she does the same thing, because I've seen her do it, and I realized that she must be bored all the time. That is the only possible reason for wanting to make every number and letter you write down perfect. The only thing I liked was reading the last chapter of *The Borrowers* and voting for our next book, which is *Johnny Tremain,* not *The Black Stallion,* but even though I made a face, *I did not say anything.*

After school, I tried something. That was to go out of the school not by the front door—which is the door I usually use, since you can go out the front door and walk down the street and there you are at my house and you can look at the bay in the distance the whole time—but by the door that goes to the playground. A lot of kids leave that way, and then cut across the playground to get home. One of these is Ruthie Creighton. I took some time putting my things away (still, you might say, doing what I was supposed to extra well), and then I walked slowly out of our room, and just followed all those kids. No one noticed me—I mean,

Marilyn Cooper asked me if I had liked *The Borrowers*, because her mom gave her a copy for her birthday, and Paulie Miller told me he was getting a puppy, but mostly I pretended I was doing what I always do, acting like I had to go to the market (where I *was* allowed to go, but only if I told someone I was going), and it didn't take too long for me to just be walking along by myself, maybe half a block behind Ruthie, who was dragging her jacket along the sidewalk and sniffling like she didn't have a tissue. I saw where she went into her house—it was a yellow house with a steep outside staircase. She went up and opened the door at the top. I waited a little while longer, but she didn't come out. I didn't see a yard or any kids in the street. I got home by a quarter to four, according to my watch, but no one said anything when I came in the house—Grandma was rocking Joan Ariel to sleep in our rocking chair (she put her finger to her lips) and Mom was upstairs taking a shower. Grandma made dinner again that night, and Grandpa came over, and we had spaghetti and meatballs.

The phone rang during dinner, and I answered it because everyone else was doing something—even

Grandpa was in the kitchen getting more bread—and it was Abby, saying that Blue was fine, but coming to their place for some turnout. I wondered how to ask my question. Finally, I said, "How is Ned?"

And she said, "He's happier. He has a new friend."

I said, "What is his name?"

She said, "Ben."

I dropped the phone, but I picked it up again. I didn't know what to think, so I decided not to think anything, and said, "That's neat. Okay, see you Saturday."

Joan Ariel wasn't old enough to sit in the high chair, or even eat anything, but Mom had a little bassinet by her own chair. She could rock it back and forth with one hand while eating her pecan tart—Grandma makes these. They are like tiny pecan pies, and everyone loves them. Mostly, everyone talked about Joan Ariel—what she did all day (sleep, eat, get her diaper changed, cry a little, get carried outside when the sun was out). Mom asked me how school was, but she yawned when I was telling her, and then smiled and said, "Wonderful, honey," which always means that she isn't listening. I picked out the pecans one by one and ate them, then scraped out the sweet filling with my spoon, then picked up the crust with my fingers and ate it like a cracker. No one said a word. Then I got up and took my plate into the kitchen without asking to be excused from the table, and no one said a word then, either. They were still talking about Joan Ariel. I looked at her. It was hard to tell if she was awake or asleep, but she wasn't meeping or cheeping.

Now that I was no longer an only child, it was easy to see that there had been two sides to being an only child, because no adult around you has anything better to do than to watch what you are doing. This can be good or bad. If they are in a good mood, then everything you do, you feel like you are on television or something, and you are always getting a laugh or some applause. If the adult is in a bad mood, though, an only child feels like she is being followed around by a big dark cloud, and every so often lightning is going to strike—"*Where* is your jacket? *What* time do you think it is? Do *not* talk to me in that tone of voice!" The good moods and the bad moods do not have a regular rhythm—they come and go. I guess I just learned to put up with it.

Now that Joan Ariel was here, it looked like I could do just about whatever I wanted. When I walked into the living room and stared for a minute at the TV, and then looked out the window at the empty street and the Clarks' house on the other side, I had to wonder what I wanted to do. For the moment, I couldn't think of anything. So I got *Misty of Chincoteague* out of my bag and sat down on the couch. That was another problem—I had been so good at school all day that my work was done, and I didn't even have anything to read, since Miss Cranfield hadn't handed out *Johnny Tremain* yet and I had read all of my own books. There's another book that I would like to read, *Black Gold*, which I have seen in the library but never checked out. It is about a racehorse from Oklahoma (so there, Mr. Lovitt). Anyway, while I was sitting there, I heard Mrs. Murphy ring her bell, and I thought maybe I should make better friends with Jimmy Murphy, because he seemed always to have something to do. I for sure did not want to end up like Kathleen Kernan. Now here came my name from the dining room—"Ellen!"—and then Mom appeared in the doorway, with Joan Ariel in her arms, and she said, "Oh, honey! Could you please help Grandma with the dishes? Grandpa wants to get home in time for Red Skelton on TV." She spoke in a very soft voice, and I saw that Joan Ariel was asleep.

After I passed her to go into the kitchen, she went very quietly through the living room and up the stairs.

Grandpa was sitting at the kitchen table. The window beside him was open and he was smoking his cigarette. I took a clean dish towel out of the drawer and started wiping the plates and stacking them on the table, since I couldn't reach high enough to put them away. Grandma said, "Thanks, sweetie," but they didn't say anything else. Once all the china was done, she said she would leave the pots and pans in the rack. Then she drained the sink, folded the dishcloth, and put the china away. She closed all the cabinets. Grandpa looked at his watch. He seemed impatient to get going. They gave me little kisses, and went out the back door. A minute later, I could hear the car start up and drive off, and then everything was quiet. I knew without anyone telling me that it had to be quiet, just so that Joan Ariel would stay asleep. I stood there for a little while, thinking about Ned, and then I went out the back door and around to the side. I looked up at Mom's window. It was dark. The whole house was dark except for the kitchen. You could hear the wind fluffing up the trees and pushing its way around the corners of the house, and I really do think that you could hear the ocean, too, five blocks down, tapping the shore, billowing, and sliding out again. It was full nighttime. The moon was already up—just a rounded sliver in the dark sky above the ocean. I decided to go for a walk—a really long walk.

Chapter 11

Even the Murphy boys have to be in by dark, and they do come in by dark. I thought about that as I passed their house—the lights were on in the living room, and I could see Mary, Jane, and Jimmy sitting on the couch. Mary had Brian on her knee. I could also hear the TV just a little—the audience laughing at something. I kept walking—down the street, the easiest way. But it didn't seem that dark. There were streetlights even on our little street, and porch lights, and two cars went by—headlights and taillights. Once I got to the corner of the biggest avenue, I turned left, crossed our little street, and then walked along. There was light everywhere, because the stores were still open, and the movie theater was all lit up, showing something called *Thoroughly Modern Millie*. I looked at the poster for a while, because I couldn't figure out much about it, but I started walking again when someone stepped out of the door of the theater and came toward me—no one I recognized, but since my family has lived here such a long time, there are a lot of people who might recognize me that I don't know. I walked like I knew where I was going, which I did. It was windier along the big avenue, and cars kept going by, so I buttoned my sweater. I said to Ned, "I am taking a walk," but I couldn't see the pasture or the trees or anything except the street and the department store up ahead, with all the doors open and people going in and out. I stayed on my side of the avenue, because about twenty people at the department store know Mom and me, and for sure they would ask me what I thought I was doing.

What did I think I was doing?

I didn't know, and that was the reason that I was enjoying myself.

I look down at my shoes. I am wearing my school shoes—saddle shoes, brown and white, which I think look good. The streetlights make the pavement a sort of dark, sparkly gray. I watch my saddle shoes stepping along, left right left right, and my socks are neatly folded down. I still have my pleated navy-blue skirt on, since I haven't changed into playclothes, and the pleats wiggle from side to side as I step. I enjoy this part for about a block, then I start looking at the shoes of the people who come toward me, then I look into the windows that I am passing. There are some toys on display at one store, but I don't want to stop, just to keep walking and walking and walking. Pretty soon, the department store is two blocks behind me, and then three. The street isn't as well lit as it was by the movie theater and the department store, and two of the streetlights are out. I don't mind that. I turn left again, because I am a little afraid of crossing the big street, even at a light, and I start up the hill.

Now that it is darker and quieter, I can see Ned a little better. He is standing not far from Ben, and they are picking up the last bits of hay that Abby threw over the fence. I don't say anything to them—instead, I imagine Mom and Dad, Miss Cranfield, Grandma and Grandpa, and Abby and her dad, too. I am saying to them, "I talk to Ned and he talks back."

Abby says, "Ned can't talk, but horses do communicate quite a few different ideas with their bodies and their whinnies."

Dad says, "Quit making stuff up."

Mom says, "She may not know that she is making anything up, but, sweetie, there is a difference sometimes between what really happens and what we think is happening."

Miss Cranfield shakes her head regretfully.

Grandma says, "Nothing in the world wrong with making things up, you ask me."

Grandpa says, "She needs her head examined, is what she needs."

Mom says, "Daddy, quit joking." And her eyebrows lower as if she is worried.

Grandma says, "Leave the child alone."

Abby says, "Horses are more intelligent than most people think they are."

Abby's dad says, in a gruff, loud voice, "It's the carrot or the stick. That's all they understand."

I kept walking. It wasn't that late—lights and TVs were on in almost every house, and when I went past the market, it was still open, which meant that it wasn't nine o'clock yet. But I didn't look at my watch.

Instead, I took it off and put it in my pocket. I thought that looking at it might make me scared in some way. The hill got steeper.

I knew that I was making things up. I knew that Ned was a horse and that horses can't talk. I knew that I have an active imagination, as Mom says. I've been talking all the time and telling stories for as long as I can remember. Here is how it is. You are saying what happened at school: Frankie Crandall threw up at his desk after lunch, and then Jane Ann Carroll, who was sitting two desks away from him, looked at him, and she threw up, too. This doesn't happen at school every week, but it does happen. So you're telling this story, except that you can't remember what was for lunch, so you say that they served brains, which they never serve, but which is a lot more likely to make someone throw up than a hot dog. So you say they served monkey brains. Then you think that if they served monkey brains, more kids would throw up, so instead of two kids throwing up, you say that five kids threw up, and that one of them, say, Jane Ann Carroll, threw up on her shoes, which makes everyone laugh. So there you are. You started out telling the truth, but then it seemed like more fun to make stuff up. I feel like that was what happened about Ned. However, if you then throw in what I was now thinking of as the Ben Question, you have to ask yourself: What if you told your mom that five kids had thrown up because they served brains in the lunchroom, and then the next day, they served brains in the lunchroom and five kids threw up, including Jane Ann Carroll on her shoes?

I kept walking, and the main thing I wanted to do now was go home and call Abby. If it was not yet nine, then Abby would for sure be up, and I could find out if the horse's name really was Ben, or if I was just thinking it was Ben when it was really Sven (Grandpa has a friend named Sven, so this was a possibility). The problem was that I was not quite sure where I was—I was farther away from home than the market, because when I was thinking about all of this, I just kept walking, the way that you do when you are thinking and thinking. I halted and looked all around. I'd probably been driven through this neighborhood lots of times, but none of the houses looked at all familiar.

I walked to the corner, crossed the street, and looked at the street sign. It said SINEX. Across the street and farther up, I could sort of see a large, dark building, and I realized that I was somewhere near the junior high school, which used to be the high school. If I was near there, then I was really far away from home. I turned around and started walking back the way I'd come, which is what they always tell you to do when you are lost.

But even I knew that I wasn't lost—I was in trouble. I walked back down the hill, turned on the street above the market (it was now closed), walked slowly past a barking dog, then came to my school playground, which was huge and extra dark (the school was dark, too—no lights in any windows), then walked around the school. Finally, at the top of our street, I took my watch out and went under the streetlight. It was twenty minutes to ten. I straightened my sweater and my socks and sort of patted my hair and pushed it out of my face, and I walked down the street and then up the steps of our house (there are only two) exactly as if I knew what I was doing, and had never done anything wrong in my life.

The lights were on in the living room, and when I turned the doorknob, the door jumped back and there was Mom in her robe, and she was fit to be tied. She had Joan Ariel in her arms, but she was also holding the phone in one of her hands. She said, in a very "I mean what I say" voice, "I was just calling the police! I thought you'd been kidnapped! Where in the world have you been?"

When a grown-up is mad at you, there are lots of ways to act. What they want you to do is say that you are sorry and will never do that again. They also want you to never tell a lie and not to have done anything wrong. Most of the time, you cannot do all of these things at the same time. The easiest thing is to tell a lie, or rather, a story, kind of like the brains, but something that might really be true. So I could have said, "I was down by the Murphys, talking to Jimmy, and I fell asleep on their porch swing because I was so tired after doing all my work today all day and paying attention every minute." But I didn't know if she'd already called the Murphys, so I couldn't try that, because if they *catch* you in a lie, then you get into about ten times more trouble than if you just did something wrong. I said, "I went for a walk and got lost."

"After dark?"

"Well, it wasn't that dark."

"Where did you go?"

"Around the block. Up to the school." All true.

"Why did you do that?"

"I didn't have anything else to do." Also true.

"Why didn't you tell me where you were going, or ask me?"

"You were asleep." True. I hadn't yet told any lies.

Now she sounded not quite as mad, and anyway, Joan Ariel started to meep and cheep. She said, "Surely, you know that you aren't allowed to go walking all over the place after dark."

I said, "I didn't know that." You can say this, but only the first time.

She gave a big sigh, shifted Joan Ariel to one arm, hung up the phone, and then sat down in the rocking chair. She clucked a few times, and finally said, "Well, for goodness' sake. Go on to bed, and we'll talk about this in the morning."

I went over and gave her a good-night kiss, then patted Joan Ariel lightly on the forehead.

Finally, I said, "I'm sorry." And I was, really. But not that sorry, because I thought our town was way more interesting in the nighttime than it was in the daytime.

As for Ned and Sven, I thought I would be patient, like they are always telling me to be, and ask Abby some questions on Saturday. And we didn't talk about my walk in the morning, because Mom and Joan Ariel were still asleep, and Grandma, who came to give me my breakfast, didn't know about it. After I'd eaten my first pancake, I said, "Does anybody ever really run away from home?"

"Used to, when my own pa was young. He said he knew a couple of boys who did. I never knew any, unless you count the ones who went to work on the fishing boats out of Monterey. They were pretty young. But it was an exciting job, so they quit school and went to work."

"Abby's brother quit school."

Grandma didn't say anything, just shook her head and gave me another pancake.

I didn't talk to Ned that night, or for the rest of the week, and I did do all my work, including reading ahead in *Johnny Tremain,* and finished the whole book by Friday.

And Mom didn't bring my walk up again, either. She would have if I were still an only child.

Chapter 12

As soon as I got up to go to my lesson on Saturday, I decided to be as good as I had ever been, because I saw something at school during the week that was very interesting. Now that I could not draw anything, talk to myself, talk to anyone else, raise my hand all the time, or even look out the window, there was nothing to do but look at the other kids, and I noticed Melanie Trevor. She wasn't sitting in the front row and she wasn't sitting in the back row, and she did raise her hand four times, and Miss Cranfield called on her three times, and I am not kidding when I say that I recognized her voice, so yes, I had seen her plenty, but I hadn't paid any attention to her. She was interesting, and she got more interesting, even though she's not pretty, she's not ugly, her hair isn't long or short, and it is not brown or blond or red, just hair. The thing I noticed about her was that she sat quietly at her desk, no fidgeting, and she looked around, but not like the other kids do, because they are bored and want something to do or because they are making faces at one another, but because she wanted to find out stuff. I suppose that she does find out stuff, too, because each time Miss Cranfield called on her, she answered the question correctly, and on Friday, when I saw that Miss Cranfield was doing some grades, I got up and went to her desk to ask her whether I could go to the bathroom, just so I could see the grade book, and there was "Melanie"—A, A, A, A, A, A. More A's than I had. Miss Cranfield saw me looking and put her hand over the paper. I went down the hall to the bathroom and stood around for a while and came back.

I was thinking I might sometime make friends with Melanie, but what I did first was wake up Saturday morning and say to myself, "Today I am Melanie." Then I practiced looking around my room at things (I hadn't noticed that my old stuffed bunny from two Easters ago had lost an eye, so there you are—I learned something). Then I got dressed in my riding clothes and went downstairs and sat down at the breakfast table. Mom had Joan Ariel propped on her shoulder, and Joan Ariel looked a little cross-eyed, then Mom put her in her bassinet, and Joan Ariel waited to scream for exactly the time it took Mom to make my scrambled egg. Then, while I was eating, she picked Joan Ariel up again, and Dad came into the kitchen, dressed but yawning, and the thing I noticed was that he was not wearing matching socks. But I didn't say anything.

Abby had told me once that even though the stables own Blue, he only gets a little "turnout" from time to time because there are so many horses there. The turnouts are small pastures without any grass, and he gets an hour. At Abby's place, he goes out all day and all night and eats off the ground and wanders around. The pastures are very big, and this year, they're still green. I was Melanie during the whole car ride out there. Dad turned around two times and looked at me. The second time, he said, "You okay?"

"Yes, why?"

"Well, you haven't said a thing. I thought maybe you'd fallen asleep."

"I am thinking."

"About what?"

"Flowers. I wish I knew the names of flowers." I didn't, really, but I didn't want to say that I was thinking about Ned.

"You can ask."

"I might."

So when we reached Abby's and got out of the car, I saw a tiny little orange flower, and I asked.

Dad said, "That's a scarlet pimpernel."

So, another thing that I knew now. I bent down and looked at it, and said those strange words, "scarlet" and "pimpernel," out loud to myself. Dad smiled and kissed me on the head. He said, "Sweetheart, you are a curious girl."

Abby was dressed in her cowboy clothes—blue jeans, and some boots, and a cowboy hat, and this shirt that I really liked, black with a red embroidered bucking bronco just below each shoulder. She was carrying two lead ropes, and we went straight to the pasture gate. It took a few minutes. When we got there, she said, "Are you okay?"

"Why?"

"You haven't said a word. You don't have a sore throat or anything, do you?"

"My teacher told me that I had to be quiet and pay attention for the rest of the school year because I was wearing her out."

Abby laughed and laughed.

Blue and Gee Whiz came to the gate as soon as Abby whistled. I petted Blue, but the one I was looking at was Ned, who was grazing with Ben on this little hill under some trees. Here are the things I saw:

Ned looked up at the whistle, and turned his head toward us, but Ben didn't.

Ned switched his tail, and then Ben switched his tail.

Ben stuck his nose into a bunch of weeds and pushed at them like he was looking for something.

A mare in the mare pasture whinnied.

Ned pricked his ears at the whinny, but didn't answer.

Gee Whiz answered, and he was really loud. My ears were ringing.

I said, "Do they have different whinnies?"

"Oh, sure," said Abby. "They can tell each other apart, and I can tell them apart, too. Gee Whiz is loud and piercing. I guess you noticed that. My horse Jack, remember him? The one at the racetrack now? His racing name is Jack So Far. He always sounds like he is whining. I call it his 'whiny.'"

"What does Ned sound like?"

"Ned hardly ever whinnies." She thought for a moment, then said, "Nope. I guess I've never heard him whinny. That's kind of strange."

"What about Ben?"

"He goes 'Eee-eee' sometimes. I'll listen."

We led Blue and Gee Whiz back to the barn and cross-tied them opposite one another. Here's what I noticed:

Blue looked this way and that, pulling at his cross-ties, but only a little.

Gee Whiz stared up the hillside with his ears pricked. I let my gaze follow his, and in a moment or two, I saw a coyote making its way along.

Blue never noticed the coyote.

Both horses were good about lifting up their front feet to have them cleaned, but when Abby picked up Gee Whiz's back feet, he sort of leaned on her. Blue didn't do that. I wondered if Gee Whiz would ever be as good a horse—as *considerate* a horse—as Blue.

When we walked them to the mounting block, Blue

stayed right with me, and if I slowed my steps a little, he slowed his.

Gee Whiz seemed to expect Abby to keep up with him.

Once we were in the arena and walking and trotting to warm up, Ned came over to the fence and watched us. I made myself ride my very best. I wanted to show Ned that someday, maybe . . .

But I dared not say it even to myself, much less out loud.

I did say, very softly, one more time, "I am Melanie."

It was a good lesson. Blue was a little tired from all the showing, but that just meant that I had to wave the crop a little to get him up into the canter, and then when he was cantering, he went around easy as you please, as if he were half-asleep. His canter is very rhythmical. I counted in my head, one two three, one two three, one two three. After about fifteen minutes, Abby said, "Are you enjoying yourself today?"

I said, "Yes." That was all. I am Melanie.

After that, Abby herself stopped talking. I guess she decided that you can say "Heels down" or "Thumbs up" or "Look where you're going" only so many times without boring yourself to death. She started doing serpentines and spirals and loops at the trot and the canter, every so often including a little cavalletti or crossbar, and Blue and I followed her as best we could. Anyway, she did not have to say "Heels down," "Thumbs up," or "Look where you're going," because I said those things to myself. And I listened to me.

We took a break and walked around. All along one side of the ring, there was another kind of flower, this one white and small. When we walked past it, the smell sort of rose around us. Because of the smell, I did say, "What's that?"

"Alyssum."

Ned stayed more or less beside that end of the arena, walking back and forth, sometimes putting his head down to snatch a tuft of something. After we did all that, Abby said, "Do you mind if you don't jump today? I think Blue is exhausted from all his lessons and show-ing at the stables. I don't want him to get sore."

Melanie said, "I don't mind."

Blue flicked his ears. He knew we were talking about him, but as much as I loved him, he had never talked to me. He would whinny if we stood in the pasture and shouted, "Blue! Blue! Where are you?" but Abby had never told me that he was answering the question. Now I wondered, and so I glanced over at Ned, and I said inside my head, "When we call out to Blue, is he answering us back?"

Ned said, "You want to know where he is. He's telling you."

I turned my head (we were trotting down the long side of the arena). Ned was still snatching at bits of something.

As I got close to Abby, I sat into my saddle, and Blue slowed to a walk, no pressure on the reins. I said, "What do you think Ned is eating?"

She looked. "Oh, chamomile, I'm sure. He loves that. My mom drinks chamomile tea. It's good. It smells good, too. Anyway, Blue is going to be here for two weeks. Next week you can jump. I'll set you some good courses."

Ned said, very softly, "Chamomile," like he was telling himself a word he didn't know.

Abby said, "You want to walk on the trail?"

And I said, in a very Melanie voice (you know, easy, soft, suggesting, not demanding), "Can Ned go along?"

Abby looked at me for a long moment, then smiled. "Why not? He's used to being ponied. They do that all the time at the track. I think he'd like to get out."

Ned said, "I would."

Gee Whiz said, "Oh, for heaven's sake." But after we got Ned out of the pasture and Abby mounted Gee Whiz and led Ned along beside him on Gee Whiz's right (that is "ponying"), Gee Whiz was pretty nice to him, and only pinned his ears if Ned got past Gee Whiz's shoulder. It was obvious to me, even though Ned didn't tell me, that Gee Whiz had to always be the winner. And that Ned didn't really care. Another interesting thing.

We walked along between the two pastures, then went through the gate, up the hill to the left, and over the ridge (not a very big ridge) onto the hillside that ran along the fence between Abby's ranch and the Jordan Ranch. We could see some cattle in the distance, but they were just plain old Black Angus, not those blue cows that had been there before. Abby's dad, I remembered, thought those blue cows were a terrible pain in the neck. The trail widened, and I let Blue come up alongside Gee Whiz on the left side (not past his shoulder, of course), and I said, "I wonder if there are any real blue horses."

"Blue roans look sort of blue, but they aren't really blue. Danny brought one home once to try out, but he

didn't like his way of moving, so he didn't keep him."
Now Gee Whiz's ears pricked again, then Blue's, then
Ned's, and there was Rusty. She appeared at the top of
the hill and looked down at us, then trotted toward us,
wagging her tail. To me, she always looked like a wolf
should look, sleek and fast. We kept walking along the
trail. It got narrower, and so I fell behind again. When
the dog got to us, she made sure that she led the way,
and Gee Whiz let her. Ned had nothing to say that I
wouldn't have known on my own, just looking around.

When we went home in the car (stopping at the
supermarket for a salami sandwich, which I needed),
I thought Melanie had done a good job, even though
being Melanie was exhausting. I went back to being
myself, but I thought about what I'd learned, and
wrote it down in my notebook before I went to bed. It
was 11:13 when I turned out my light.

Chapter 13

On Monday, as soon as I got to school, I started watching Melanie again—so much that I noticed Miss Cranfield looking at me when she asked questions as if she was wondering why I wasn't raising my hand. When she did look at me, I would stop looking at Melanie and look at the board, or at my desk, following instructions *all the time.* I told myself I could stop if I wanted to, so I kept going.

One thing I saw was that Melanie would smile sometimes at Ruthie Creighton, and Ruthie would smile back. This happened three times in the morning. At lunch, I was sitting with Todd and Ann, and Todd was telling a moron joke. Ann said that if he knew that he himself was a moron, then he wouldn't tell those jokes, because they were stupid. This made Todd laugh, because he always laughs, even when the joke is on him. I looked across the lunchroom at Melanie, who was eating what they served, and Ruthie. Ruthie was not sitting at Melanie's table—she was sitting alone, as usual, and she had something wrapped in brown paper. Something small. She started opening the paper, and then Melanie turned and said something to her, and then Ruthie held out her hand and Melanie gave her an orange. Ruthie smiled. It was a pretty smile. Something else I learned. But then Melanie turned back to her own lunch, and they didn't talk about anything. I decided that Melanie was one of those girls that my grandmother would call "deep as a well and twice as dark." Then my grandma would shake her head. She likes people who talk. That's why she likes me.

After lunch, Todd and Ann and I went out to the playground. Todd could get teased for sitting with us at lunch, but he's the only kid our age who can walk along the top railing of the jungle gym, and he does it pretty often, when none of the teachers are looking. One time in the fall, a teacher saw him and fainted. Well, that's what I say. Probably she yelled at him, but by the time I had told everyone that she'd fainted, I could see her fainting perfectly well, just going *"Ohhhh!"* and slumping to the side. Today, Ann was talking about something and I wasn't paying any attention, because I wanted to walk past the swings to the hopscotch area. I could see Melanie there, by herself. I didn't see Ruthie anywhere. I walked straight over to Melanie and said, "Can we play?"

Melanie nodded.

I went to the edge of the playground and found two pebbles and handed one to Ann, and we went back to the hopscotch court, which was painted on the pavement. There were two of them—one had three hops that came first, and one had hop, jump, hop. Melanie was playing the three-hop one, and she was pretty good.

There are people who don't know the rules of hopscotch, most of them boys. What you do is, you toss the pebble into the first of the squares (1 to 10), and then you jump over that square as you hop and jump to the far end, then you jump and spin (usually on two feet, but sometimes on one), and then you hop and jump back to where your pebble is. You bend down and pick it up, then start over with square 2, and so on. You ask me, it is a kind of ballet, and that is what Melanie made it look like. She got through the third square without a mistake, and the mistake she made after that was throwing the pebble a little too straight so that it landed in 5 instead of 4, just over the line. Ann went next. She got to 2. She's not a very good hopper, though she can jump and spin high. Normally, I would have kept talking the whole time I was hopping and jumping. I think telling yourself what to do always works. But I pressed my lips shut and did the best I could. I made it through 1 and 2, but I felt wobbly the whole time. For 3, I didn't throw the pebble very hard and it landed in 2. I did it on purpose, because I was exhausted.

Now Melanie went. Ann, not me, said, "Do you take dancing lessons?"

"Yes," said Melanie.

"Where?" said Ann.

"At a studio in Monterey. My mom did ballet when she was young, but she got too tall. I'm going to get too tall, too, but it's fun for now."

I said, "You should take riding lessons."

Melanie looked at me, but didn't smile or say anything. She concentrated, and got to square 8. We were never going to beat her.

I closed my eyes.

Ned said, "Look where you're going, but not at your feet." He was standing under the tree. Ben was behind him, reaching his head around to scratch his hip. He snorted and shook his ears. I opened my eyes. It was a lot cloudier on our playground than it was in Ned's pasture.

Ann was standing up straight, facing the street. She gave a little "Huh," jumped, and spun. She made it. She jumped and hopped back to the beginning, picking her pebble up on the way. Altogether, she made it to square 5.

I put my pebble between my thumb and first two fingers and stared at the painted 3, then tossed the pebble without looking at it. It landed on the 3. Now I hopped, 1, 2, and over 3, landed on both feet in 4 and 5, hopped into 6, landed on both feet in 7 and 8, hopped into 9 and then 10, which is "home"—once you hop into 10, you can put both feet down and jump and spin. The whole time, I sort of looked up and sort of looked down—I could see the squares out of the bottom of my eyes, but I could also see the air and the fence and the street. Coming back, I did the same, looking at the squares, but also at the playground and the school. It was a relief to bend down in 4 and 5 and pick up my pebble in 3, then hop hop hop home. I was happy and impressed, but to Ann and Melanie, it was all the same as usual. I got through 4 and 5, and then the school bell rang, and we went back to class. Melanie walked along with us, smiling, but she didn't say anything—it was like it never occurred to her to talk. Ann said that she and her mom were going to bake a pie after school, lemon meringue.

That afternoon, I looked for all the world as if I were paying attention, but mostly I was thinking about that feeling I'd had playing hopscotch. I can always do two things at once, no matter what the grown-ups say.

Having Joan Ariel around was pretty interesting, too. I'd never heard any of the Murphys say that their brothers or sisters were interesting. Jimmy Murphy said that his sisters drove him crazy. Mary and Jane, who had to babysit, would just stand there with their arms crossed and scowl at Brian, waiting for him to do something naughty or dangerous. Joan Ariel made all sorts of faces. Sometimes she cried—her face would bunch up and then her mouth would open really wide, and you could see all the way down her throat. She was not screaming like a Murphy, but it wasn't meep-meeping anymore, either. Whatever Mom was doing, she would drop it and jump to her feet. She didn't always pick Joan Ariel up—sometimes she just walked back and forth waiting for the right time to give her a bottle. Grandma said give it to her when she wants it, but Mom had a book that said wait until the right time. There were a few days after Mom and Grandma had a "discussion" about this when Grandma didn't come over, but then she started in again, and they agreed that when Mom was there, they would do it Mom's way, and when Grandma was by herself, she could do whatever she wanted. Mom was pretty much always there, though. Joan Ariel was now three weeks old. Mom said that she would start smiling at six weeks, and I didn't say anything, but sometimes Joan Ariel already looked like she was smiling—her mouth would open and her lips would spread, and she would stare at me with her eyes crossed. I would then make a face, just for practice. Sometimes when I made lots of faces, she stared at me and didn't cry at all. She still didn't know the difference between night and day—sometimes she would be up at night and sleep in the day, and other times she would be up most of the day and sleep in the night. Mom might still be wearing her robe when I got home from school, but other times she would meet me at school with the baby carriage, and we would take Joan Ariel for a walk. Twice, Miss Cranfield saw us and came over, leaned into the baby carriage, and cooed at Joan Ariel—how was she doing, was she sleeping through the night? Then Miss Cranfield looked at me, and I understood that she knows that I know that she knows that I know that I have to be good for the rest of the year.

The Wednesday after Ann and I played hopscotch with Melanie, Mom and Joan Ariel and I walked around the block and right past Ruthie Creighton's house. It was a sunny day, Joan Ariel was sleeping and meeping, Mom was humming to herself, and I was singing a song Jimmy Murphy had taught me: "Left right left right I left my wife with forty-six children alone in the kitchen in a starving condition with nothing but gingerbread left right left." It doesn't have much of a tune. Every time Jimmy Murphy sings it, it makes me laugh. We crossed the street by Ruthie's house, and Mom sped up. Ruthie was sitting on the top step of the outside staircase. She wasn't doing anything. She looked right at me, and I looked right at her. Mom clucked. We passed Ruthie, and she clucked again. When we got to the next corner and turned left, I said, "What?"

Mom said, "You know, when I was growing up, I had to say 'ma'am' and 'sir.' Every time my parents would ask me a question, I would have to say 'Yes, ma'am' or 'No, sir.'"

I waited to hear something about how this had made her into who she was today, but she just looked down at me and sighed, then said, "That poor girl."

"Does she have to say 'ma'am' and 'sir' all the time?"

Mom stopped, put her hands on her hips, and looked at me, then laughed all of a sudden and said, "Oh, Ellen, you are one of a kind."

We walked on, but after a step or two, Mom looked back, then said, "No, no. Her dad, that's Albert Creighton, embezzled some money, and when they dis-covered it, he ran off. That was two Christmases ago. I don't know how her mom supports the two of them. And it wasn't a lot of money. Maybe twenty-five hun-dred dollars." She clucked again and shook her head, and we crossed the next street. I had never heard the word "embezzled" before, but I knew it was something like stealing, probably without a gun or a bandanna tied over your mouth. Outlaws on horseback were always holding people up on TV, especially stagecoaches. I didn't notice much about them, even if there was some screaming. I was always looking at the horses.

When we were almost home, I said, "Well, Ruthie needs a pair of shoes, because the sole of her left one is always flapping. She tripped and fell down the other day." She didn't, as far as I knew, but she always looked like she was going to, and anyway, she did have a scrape on her knee right after Easter.

"Poor girl," Mom said again.

"Melanie Trevor gave her an orange Monday."

"You could take a little something extra in your lunch bag."

"You mean I don't have to eat school lunch anymore?"

She looked at me, then said, "I guess not."

And then, right at the same time, I said, "Can I have peanut butter and jelly every day?" and she said, "You cannot have peanut butter and jelly every day."

But the next day, Mom was still in bed when it came time to go to school, so I made my own lunch, and it was peanut butter and jelly (two sandwiches, one for me and one for Ruthie) and two of Grandma's oatmeal cookies and an orange (for Ruthie) and a strip of red licorice (for me). It was a big peanut butter day, because Todd said at morning recess that he had crunchy peanut butter and bacon, and Ann said she had salami and a peanut butter cup. The real question was how to get the sandwich, the orange, and the cookie to Ruthie. On the way to the lunchroom, I realized that the answer was Melanie, especially since you didn't have to make small talk with her, so I let Todd and Ann walk ahead and loitered around waiting for her. She was slow. I assumed that she was doing something good like straightening her desk or making sure her shoes were tied with double knots. But eventually she came along, and I walked beside her. We didn't say anything until we were almost to the lunchroom, which is down some stairs and around a corner. I tried very very hard not to say a word, but it seemed like the words were popping in my mouth, so I finally let a few out. I said, "I made some lunch for Ruthie."

"She won't take it. It took me a month to get her to take an orange sometimes."

"Why won't she take it?"

"It makes people look at her. What's the lunch?"

"Peanut butter and jelly. An oatmeal cookie. An orange."

We were now inside the lunchroom. Melanie

stopped and looked around in her Melanie way. If she were a horse, her ears would have been pricked. She said, "Do you have a pencil?"

I did. She held out her hand. I gave her the pencil. She kept holding out her hand, so I gave her the bag. She wrote FOR RUTHIE on the bag, then set it on the table where Ruthie always sat. I said, "Will she take it?"

Melanie said, "Maybe, maybe not. It's up to her." She put her hand on my arm and moved me away from the table. It was like some food for a wild animal. You just had to hope that she would sniff it and not run away. Melanie sat with Todd and Ann and me for lunch. Ann talked about the lemon meringue pie, which she had been talking about all week (yes, she had whipped the egg whites), and Todd said that a boy in his friend's class had gone to sleep during multiplication and fallen out of his seat. He didn't even wake up then, so Mr. Casey had everyone stand up and call out, "One times one is one, two times two is four, three times three is nine. . . ." The boy woke up at three and had to sit on the floor all the way up to the tens. Melanie didn't say anything. We couldn't see the bag, but we saw on the way out to the playground that it was gone.

Chapter 14

Abby always keeps her promises, so when I showed up for my lesson Saturday, the arena was full of jumps, all bright colors and perfect footing. Some of the jumps were low and some were high, and I pretended that I was going to get on Gee Whiz and jump the high ones, and then I pretended that I was not going to do that. Instead, I was going to get on Ned and jump the high ones—and then came the real surprise, because before my lesson on Blue, Abby said, "Let's do something." She gave me a lead rope and took one herself, and we walked to the pasture. We patted Blue and Gee Whiz, but we walked right past them, over to Ned and Ben. We snapped the lead ropes on to their halters. Abby led the way with Ben, and I followed with Ned. Ned was saying, "Oh boy. I've been waiting for this." He walked nicely, for a young horse. Ben wasn't as good, but Abby did what she always does—she acted like she wasn't paying a bit of attention to him while in the meantime making him stop and turn and behave himself.

In the arena, Abby had built a jumping chute— I hadn't seen it at first because it was along the far side. There was a long line of green and blue poles set up on standards so that they were parallel to the railing of the arena. That was the "chute," but instead of jumps set up across the chute, there were only a couple of poles on the ground. We unsnapped the lead ropes and let Ned and Ben snort and play in the arena. They trotted around together, pinning their ears at each other and kicking up, backing off from the jump standards and pretending to be frightened, then galloping away. The funny thing was that after about five minutes of this, Gee Whiz let out a whinny from the pasture that was so loud it was almost a scream. It was like he was saying, "Settle down, you idiots!" because they snorted and took some deep breaths and started walking around, just looking at things, and pretty soon they sighed and came over to us, first Ned, then Ben. Abby had handed me a piece of carrot, which I gave to Ned while she gave a piece to Ben. We snapped the lead ropes back on, then walked the horses down through the jumping chute and over the poles, but other places, too. Abby's dog sat on the hillside watching us for a while, then trotted away toward the house and the road. The next funny thing was that a coyote came along, right where Abby's dog had been, easy as you please. It sat down and scratched its neck. It looked at us, and the horses looked up at it. I pointed it out, and Abby said, "Good-looking. Nice coat. Must be a young one."

Now she handed me some lumps of sugar and told me to stand at one end of the jumping chute. She took Ned to the other end, put him inside the chute, then unsnapped the lead rope. She didn't smack him or any-thing, but she didn't let him go out of the chute. She kept telling him something, but the wind was blowing from me to her, so I couldn't hear what she was say-ing. She also kept pointing him toward me. Finally, he looked at me and said, "Do you have a treat?" and I said, "Yes," and he came trotting toward me, and he trotted right over the poles. I gave him his sugar and sent him out of the chute. Ben seemed dumber. He saw the poles and snorted at them. For a few minutes, it looked like he wasn't going to go near them for all the tea in China, as my grandmother would say. Then he went close to them. This time, Abby did smack him with the end of the lead rope, and he jumped over the first one like it was on fire, then snorted at the second one and jumped high over that one, too. When he got to me and I gave him the treat, he acted like he was feeling lucky to be alive. But he didn't say anything.

Now Abby and I switched places. As soon as I got to the other end, Ned came trotting toward me over the poles. He didn't touch them with even the tip of a single toe. Ben had learned something the first time through—this time he hesitated, but then he went. He didn't act like the poles were on fire, but he acted like they could burst into flames at any moment. It took him four times to learn what Ned learned the first time. Abby set the two poles up as a crossbar, pretty low, but still high enough so that the horses would have to do something. What happened next was one of the most interesting things I ever saw in my life.

In a jumping chute, the fence side and the pole side are as far apart as the jump is wide, so that the horse has no way of going around the jump. Some horses really want to go around the jump; others don't care. When Abby had Sophia's horse Onyx, he would see a jump and go for it, just for fun, but most horses don't.

Abby snapped the lead rope on to Ben, and told me to take him outside the jumping chute, but to stand not far from the crossbar, facing it. I did that. He had run around enough so that he was willing to stand still. I knew she wanted him to watch Ned, and why not? Horses learn from each other all the time—sometimes good things, sometimes bad things.

She took Ned to the other end of the chute, said something to him, and tickled him with the whip she had picked up, and he trotted, then cantered, four strides, then popped over the crossbar. Abby clapped, shouted "Good boy!" then whistled, and Ned turned and trotted, then jumped back toward her. It was so easy for him that she came straight to the jump and set it up as a regular jump, one pole across at about a foot and a half, and one pole as the ground line. Then she walked back to the beginning of the chute. He sniffed the jump, then followed her. She took his halter, turned him toward the jump, and said whatever it was that she had been saying, and he trotted two strides, then cantered two strides and lifted himself gracefully over the little jump, bending his knees, putting his nose down just a bit, then cantered off. He got past the far end of the chute, but when she whistled, he turned around and jumped it going the other way exactly as he had done it the first time. She patted him, gave him his bit of carrot, and kissed him on the nose. I had never seen her kiss a horse before.

Ben looked this way and that—at Ned, at Abby, at the jump, up the hillside, at the pasture. Miss Cranfield would have said, "Ben! Attention, please!" But I didn't say anything and neither did he. Abby brought Ned over, and we traded horses. Ned watched her walk away with Ben. I said to Ned, "You were great!"

He said, "That's all? I want to do more."

I said, "You are only four."

"A racehorse can be a champion at *three*."

I knew this was true, because my dad had been talking about the Kentucky Derby. There was a horse entered, named Damascus, who he thought was going to win. I liked that name, Damascus. All the horses in the Kentucky Derby are three.

I was pretty excited about what Ned had done, and between you and me, I thought being a jumper or a hunter was much better than being a racehorse any day, but I didn't say that to Ned. Abby had set the jump back to a crossbar, and now she pointed Ben toward it. He started trotting with this look on his face that said, "Okay, if you say so. I am doing my best." He trotted and kept trotting, and when he got to the poles, he kept trotting, and knocked them down. Then he went over to the corner of the arena and stood there breathing kind of hard. He didn't try to run away when Abby went and caught him, then set the crossbar up again, took him back to where he had started the first time, and sent him again. This time, he trotted and trotted, but when he got to the jump, he tried to bend his knees more. He kept trotting, but with higher steps. Knocked the poles down again.

Ned said, "You donkey."

Ben flicked his ears, trotted into the corner, and waited for Abby. She set the crossbar and went to him, took him back to the starting point. They stood there for a minute or two. As far as I could tell, Ned didn't say anything, but he was watching. Finally, Abby let Ben go. He trotted two steps, and then he got this look on his face like he had figured it out, and he started cantering, and he lifted his front end and his back end, got nicely over the jump, then he cantered two strides, and then he leapt and bucked and squealed past the corner and about halfway around the arena. The exciting part for me was not only that he did it, but that I was standing right there and saw a horse learn something. Abby sent Ben over the crossbar and then the little jump several more times, and every time, Ben did it right. He learned it and he didn't forget it, and he was happy. At the very end, she let Ned do it each way one more time, and then we walked the horses out for ten minutes, put them back in the pasture, and took down the jumping chute.

After that, we tacked up Blue and Gee Whiz and went into the arena and did our usual things—circles, serpentines, figure eights, walk, trot, canter. Blue behaved himself perfectly, but I thought that even if he had been a little naughty (he is never really naughty), I wouldn't have minded because I was still so happy from seeing Ned and Ben. While we were walking, before we started jumping, I said to Abby, "What was Blue like when he was learning to jump?"

"A little spooky but willing. Once he knew what he was doing, he would sometimes look down at the jump like he thought a ghost could pop out of it, but then

I realized that I was looking down at the jump just the same way, so I made myself look up and go. He got better after that. Now he's completely reliable. But some horses don't like new things, and some horses just don't care. They are all different."

"What about Ned?"

"He doesn't mind new things, as long as you give him a moment to figure them out. What he hates is horses being wild. It's like he was an only child, and so he doesn't really know what to do with other kids, because he didn't know any other kids until he got to kindergarten." Then she looked at me, and I knew she was thinking, "Uh-oh, I'm talking to an only child."

I said, "Well, if there aren't so many kids around, you learn other stuff."

She smiled and said, "I'm sure that's true!" Then she trotted away, and Blue and I followed Gee Whiz around the arena to the far end, away from the gate. Abby dismounted and ran Gee Whiz's stirrups up, and after that it was all business. She had set the jumps so that I could do three different courses. The first one was a figure eight of six jumps—we started going right, first jump, second jump, third at the far end. Then when we crossed through the center, we went between the two jumps of the three-stride that we took, then went around to the left and jumped the fourth jump, then came around over the fifth and sixth and down to the trot. The second course was three jumps in what had been the jumping chute, then around the end of the arena and over the three-stride again, then over a little wall, around in a loop, and back over the little wall. Blue did all of these perfectly, and I knew what it was like to be going along for the ride. The last course was kind of an optical illusion, and was the hardest. Abby had to explain it to me twice before I saw it— an inward spiral of four jumps, then a turn, and three more jumps along the rail. She said it was a course she had seen Sophia do with Colonel Hawkins at the stables. You would never do it in a horse show, but she and Sophia both thought you could really learn some-thing from it. I didn't say anything, but I felt nervous, especially since we went to the left, Blue's not-so-good side. My heart was pounding a little when we started. But it was easy and fun. I just kept my left rein a little tighter and my left leg a little in his side so that he would bend, and then after he went over the fourth jump and it was time to turn right, I looked at the next jump, and it was like he uncurled, switched leads without even thinking about it, and cantered over the last three jumps. Then he dropped to an easy trot and went straight to Abby, who gave him a treat, and gave me a big smile. After that, Blue and I walked around while Abby and Gee Whiz jumped a few jumps, too. It was so clear that Gee Whiz could jump anything and wanted to jump everything, but they were taking it easy. At the very end, she jumped the little wall and then went to the right over a big oxer, maybe four feet, and Gee Whiz just took a deep breath and leapt into the sky. Afterward, when they came down to the trot, he tossed his head and snorted. We walked around. I wanted to go on the trail, but I saw that my dad, who had gone into town to do some shopping at this really good grocery store they have there, was back and ready to go home. As we were walking Blue and Gee Whiz to the pasture, Abby said, "Do you remember when you threw yourself off the pony to show your mom that falling off wasn't so terrible?"

"I don't do that anymore."

"No, because you won, didn't you? But anyway, I only bring that up to say that you have gotten good, and you knew you would."

We led the horses into the pasture, turned them around, took their halters off, patted them on the neck, and walked out. Abby chained the gate. I went over to her, got up on my tiptoes, and gave her a kiss on the cheek.

Chapter 15

It is very boring doing what you're told all the time. The days seem to go by slowly slowly slowly. In the week after my lesson, I helped with the dishes, rocked Joan Ariel in her cradle (and tickled the bottoms of her feet, which she seemed to like), did all my homework, sat quietly in my seat at school, ate my lunch, left a cookie or a piece of fruit on a napkin on Ruthie Creighton's table every day, counted to a hundred between the times I raised my hand in class, smiled at Miss Cranfield, and kept my eyes down when I saw Jimmy Murphy throwing spitballs and some of the girls passing notes. I did watch Melanie, and I decided that the best way to think about her was that she came from a different planet, a very good planet, and that she was visiting Earth and writing a report that she would take back to her home planet. This was a fun way to think of her, because I could imagine the planet, and the ship, and what she really looked like when she wasn't pretending to be human, and on and on, which passed the time.

My dad was gone from Monday until late Wednesday night, and when I got up Thursday, he was sitting at the kitchen table, drinking his coffee. He looked like he was in a pretty good mood, which meant that he must have sold some vacuum cleaners, and when Mom came down with Joan Ariel, he took her on his knee and said, "Joanie girl, who do you think is going to win the Kentucky Derby?"

I finished chewing my piece of toast because a good girl does not talk with her mouth full, then said, "Why are you asking *her*?"

"Just joking around. Who do you think is going to win?"

"I hope it's Damascus. I love that name."

Dad said, "He is a good horse. You never know if their luck will hold, though."

I went up the stairs, got dressed, and walked backward to school. It was May now—the clouds floated around in the blue sky, but the fog was out before I woke up. The bay was smooth and pale, and there were three sailboats in the distance and lots of birds whooshing up and down. I had two days of school left in the week. I felt good, even though it seemed like those two days were going to last the rest of my life.

Of course, if you want bad, it has to be a boy, and as soon as I got to school, I saw that someone had been very very bad. Our school is red and white—mostly brick, with white window frames and steps and doors. It's pretty, for a school. But sometime after the teachers left the day before, and before anyone got there this morning, someone had climbed the fence and spray-painted faces on the doors and the windows in green and black. Some of the faces were smiling and some were screaming, and beside them, the person had written HA HA HA HA in three places. There were also some exclamation points. The painting was all along the front of the school, where you could see it from the street.

It took a long time to get everyone into their classrooms, and then a long time for everyone to sit down and be quiet. I don't know why we were pretty excited, but we were. Miss Cranfield kept slapping her ruler on her desk and calling out, "Silence! Sit down!" Then, after we sat down, she told us about how destroying public property is a crime and also an insult and also ugly. I personally would not have used the word "destroy," since the school was still standing, but I clasped my hands together and kept my mouth shut.

After a while, everything settled down, but when we were doing division, the classroom door opened, and the principal, Mr. Gretzky, and another man came in. They went over to Miss Cranfield and whispered, then they stood there frowning while she turned to us and said, "Children, we are going to get back to arithmetic in a few minutes, but for now, I want you all to sit up in your seats, put away your books and papers, and then place your hands on your desks, palms down." This took a couple of minutes, but then we were dead quiet, and Mr. Gretzky and the other man walked along the rows of desks, looking at our hands. I knew what they were looking for, and it was not bitten nails. My dad painted our house about two years ago, and no matter how many times he washed his hands with turpentine and all of that, he still had paint under his nails and in those edges where your nails go into your fingertips. After looking at all of our hands, Mr. Gretzky and the other man thanked Miss Cranfield and left the room. Why they thanked her, I have no idea. I looked at Jimmy Murphy and his usual spitball-throwing friend, Brad Caswell. They are in fourth grade, so even if they wanted to, they could not paint the front of the school. Even if Mrs. Murphy had no idea what Jimmy was doing half the time, she would have known if he wasn't home for dinner, or went out after dinner. But I imagined looking out our front window and seeing Jimmy and Brad hiking up the street with paint cans. It was fun to imagine, and it made me smile.

After school, when Mom came with Joan Ariel in the baby carriage, she clucked and clucked about the damage. She put her hands on her hips and shook her head, but she was smiling a little. The faces did make you smile and even laugh. They looked happy. But Mom and I pretended that it was such a scandal, as Grandma would say, and went on around the block. I said that maybe it was watercolors, and would wash away if it happened to rain (it was a little cloudy), and Mom said that they don't put watercolors in spray cans, and Joan Ariel meeped and meeped as if she was very happy, and then we had fried chicken with mashed potatoes and gravy, and so that day passed much more quickly than the days before.

Friday morning was back to normal, and I was back to being good good good. In our reading group, we got to vote on the last book of the year, and we voted for *Black Beauty*, and Miss Cranfield said that it would be sad, but actually, all the books we read were pretty sad, but not as sad as, say, "Rock-a-bye, baby, in the treetop." We got some free time before lunch, which we always got on Friday, and I started reading *Black Beauty*, and I discovered that it is not only about a horse, but about a horse who talks.

After lunch, it went around that the kids who did the painting were in seventh grade—at the junior high—and only one of them, Ralphie Short, who really was short, had gone to our school. Last year, he somehow put a big wad of gum on the piano bench on the stage in the auditorium (which is also the lunchroom), and when Miss Harrison, who is the music teacher, stood up after playing "America the Beautiful" so that we could sing along, her skirt stuck to the bench and ripped. When I told my dad about this, he said that when he was a boy, if anyone did something like that, they would be whipped, but Ralphie just had to pay for the skirt, and I guess he did not learn his lesson. He and the other two boys were going to spend the weekend with some painters scrubbing down the doors and the windows. I knew I could walk up the street and watch them, and I thought maybe I would.

And so the week passed, and here I was, on Friday night, lying in my bed in the dark, with the window open, smelling some nice things from the garden, including some roses and some jasmine and some cut grass. My door was partly open, and I could hear Mom talking to Joan Ariel in her room across the hall, and also that Dad had the TV on downstairs. The night sky at the top of my window, above the trees, was clear, and I could see some stars, a few bright ones, but only the brightest, because the moon was up there, too. I took some deep breaths and closed my eyes just a little, and then Ned walked over and said, "Hello."

I said, "Hello."

Ned said, "Are you coming tomorrow?"

"Yes, but maybe for the last time, because Blue is going back to the stables on Monday."

"He doesn't like it there."

"Why not?" I thought he was going to say something about the stalls or the turnout, but he said, "It's cold.

They clipped him all over, and then they put a blanket on him, so he is always cold or hot, never just right."

"Did you ever wear a blanket?"

"At the racetrack, there are all kinds of blankets, but they are mostly to keep you clean. I prefer to keep clean by rolling in the grass."

"Who doesn't?" shouted Gee Whiz.

"He is always butting in," said Ned. "Someone kicked him right on the haunch."

"Who?" I said.

"Blue."

I stuck this in my brain very carefully so that I would be sure to ask Abby if this was true. "Is he hurt?"

"He limped around for a day, but he was just showing off. Today he was galloping all over and bucking and kicking up, but he did stay away from Blue."

I said, "So even an old horse can learn a lesson?"

"Horses learn lessons all the time."

"I saw Ben learn some lessons the other day."

"He has to do it to know how to do it. He doesn't see very well."

"What does that mean?"

"Well, you watch him. When he isn't eating, he is looking up the hill or over at the mares or toward the house. He sees all of those things really well, but when I say, 'Oh, do you see that snake?' or 'Do you see that vulture?' he never knows what I'm talking about. He had to go over those poles with his body in order to figure it out, but he does it a few times and then he understands it all completely."

"He's farsighted."

"Huh," said Ned. "I will tell him."

"My dad is farsighted. He wears glasses." The thought of Ben wearing glasses made me laugh. I barked one laugh, then slid under the covers and put the corner of the pillow in my mouth so that Mom wouldn't hear me and come in and tell me it was ten-forty-five or something.

Ned was still there. I said, "You were really good."

"It was easy. Gee Whiz says that if you can gallop, you can jump. Ben says that, too, but you have to feel the jump."

"What do you say?"

"I say no big deal, but it is fun. I saw there were bigger jumps in there."

I said, "Someday."

And then I went to sleep, just like falling into a hole. I didn't even have a dream, and then I woke up at dawn because there was a bee buzzing around my head from the open window. The first thing I thought was that it was Saturday and this was maybe the last time I was going to see Ned, because in addition to the fact that Blue was going back to the stables, Dad and Mom were both getting a little annoyed with how far it was to Abby's ranch. It was pretty clear that my days of being spoiled were numbered, as Grandpa would say. I got up and made my bed, because even though being good is boring, you can see wherever you look that doing everything you are told to do before you are told to do it leads to at least a little more spoiling, and I needed as much as I could get.

Chapter 16

It should've been a sunny day at the ranch and a gloomy day at our house, but for once, things were reversed. Dad kept talking about this while we drove, as if the weather were the most amazing thing there is. He kept saying, "I knew you should have brought a sweater. Around here, you never know what you're going to find. And you can't believe the forecasters, either. They are just talking through their hats."

Not only was it chilly, it was windy. Every time we passed some trees, I could see them bending over a little bit and their leaves shaking. Things skittered across the road in front of us. This, of course, led Dad to talk about the tornadoes back east. He had never been in one, but he had a cousin in St. Louis, and a tornado went down the street that his street turned onto, right down it like a railroad train, but the curtains didn't even ruffle at the cousin's house. It was nighttime, he couldn't see anything, and he couldn't figure out what that noise was. Dad said that he wouldn't mind seeing a tornado someday, at least from a distance. There were people in Texas who chased tornadoes in their cars, could I imagine that?

I said, "No," because in fact I had never even seen a picture of a tornado, and so I didn't know what in the world he was talking about.

He dropped me outside of the gate and went into town to have the oil in the car changed.

Abby wasn't wearing a sweater, but she did have her sleeves down, and she had her hard hat on to keep her hair out of her face. She wasn't paying much attention to me, and was talking too fast, and so when we were tacking up, I said, "Is something bad happening?"

"No."

"You were happier last week."

"I was happy last week, that's true."

"Did something happen?"

"Not yet."

Now I stopped right where I was standing and put my hands on my hips and gave Abby a look, and she laughed out loud and said, "You are way too short for that, but it is funny. Anyway, my Jack is running in his first race today."

"The Kentucky Derby?"

"No! My heavens!" She laughed again. "Just a maiden handicap, the second race of the day, when exactly no one is there to watch. They were going to run him next week, but decided he was ready, so they entered him."

"When is post time?"

"What do you know about post time?"

"Nothing, but my dad said that post time for the Derby in Kentucky is five-twenty, which is two-twenty here, and he wants to be sure to watch it."

She handed me the lead rope, and we walked toward the pasture. The trees were rattling so hard you could hear the branches creak, and the hay that the horses hadn't yet eaten was ruffling in the grass. I straightened my shoulders and started taking bigger steps, as if I didn't care a thing about the weather.

Abby said, "He's the favorite."

I knew what that meant. I said, "Did you bet on him?"

"We don't bet. My dad says having horses is a big enough bet. You don't have to waste your money by giving it to the bookies."

"What are bookies?"

"They're the people who take the bets. I guess they keep some of the money. My dad says they keep a lot of the money."

I had no idea what she was talking about. So I said, "Well, I hope he wins," and Ned said, "I doubt it."

Ned was on the other side of the fence, and he was looking at me.

I said, "Did your Jack and Ned ever know each other?"

"Not here. I don't think at the track, because Ned came here before Jack left the training farm."

I said to Ned, "Be nice."

He flicked his ears.

We opened the gate. I shouted, "Blue, Blue, where are you?" He lifted his head, whinnied, and turned toward us, but Gee Whiz, who was pretty far behind him, came running. He was running fast, too. Another thing to make me scared. Abby said, "Stand absolutely still. He will stop."

And he did, a sliding halt to right in front of Abby. She patted him and gave him a sugar cube. She said, "He likes to do that."

Blue, of course, was much more considerate. He ambled over, took a few strokes along the neck, and pretended that he didn't know I had treats, that he was just glad to see me. Abby said, "He's going back to the stables on Monday, so we'll have the lesson there next week."

We snapped on the lead ropes and walked the horses out of the pasture. I asked my question: "Did Gee Whiz maybe get kicked this week?"

She glanced at me, then said, "I don't think so. Why do you ask?"

I didn't answer. Blue, as usual, said nothing.

Blue and Gee Whiz were grown-up horses, and they were not acting silly or afraid, but because of the wind, they were picking up their feet, pricking their ears, snorting a little bit, looking around. They were, in fact, acting the way horses do out at the stables. Jane told me once that horses who come from places like

LA tend to get extra excited when they come to the big show at the stables, and their trainers have to be prepared. It crossed my mind to wonder if Abby was prepared.

That had never crossed my mind before.

I said, "Where's your dad and your mom? I never see them."

"Dad is doing something over at the Jordan Ranch, maybe some branding. Mom went into town."

"How will you find out about the race?"

"The trainer's going to call me."

"Too bad you can't watch it on TV."

"We don't have a TV. But I wouldn't want to watch it anyway."

I didn't ask why.

We brushed the horses down, tacked them up, and led them to the mounting block. Abby waited for me to get on, but she didn't hold Blue's reins—I'm too old for that. I climbed the mounting block and pulled down the stirrup. The very next thing that happened was that I fell right off the mounting block on my butt. I sat there for a moment or two. Blue was looking down at me. And guess what? I started to cry. Maybe I haven't cried since I was a baby, because I hate to cry. Abby came over and held out her hand. She said, "Are you okay?"

But I pushed her hand away and got to my feet, then climbed the mounting block again. This is how good Blue is—he never moved.

Abby mounted, and we walked toward the arena. The wind was still blowing, and the trees were still rattling and creaking, and the clouds were still scudding through the sky, and the birds were still skating through the same sky. The wind dried the tears on my cheeks—I could feel them there—but here is the funny thing. I was not scared anymore; I was too mad at myself for being such a dunce. I gave Blue a little kick, both sides, both heels, and made him walk ahead of Gee Whiz. I never looked back, and Abby followed me into the arena. It was me that closed the gate.

Abby didn't have to say anything. I rode Blue at the walk, trot, and canter in circles and serpentines and U-turns. We halted and did transitions, and backed up and went forward, and even did a turn on the forehand in each direction. Why would she have to tell me what to do? She'd told me what to do so many times that I knew what to do. It was just like school. For a few weeks, I'd been very very good, but Miss Cranfield repeats herself and repeats herself, and it is not my fault that Jimmy Murphy and Todd and all the others aren't listening. It's also not my business that Melanie doesn't mind listening to the same thing over and over, but between you and me, why do I have to be bored most of the time? Why can't I finish my jobs and then do what I want? I imagined myself saying this to Miss Cranfield on Monday. I could feel myself scowling.

I have to admit that I asked more of Blue than I usually do. Usually, I let him go along mostly as he wants to, and he's always agreeable, if a little slow. Once in a while, I've carried a crop, and sometimes I've waved it, but I never hit him with it. Today, I wasn't carrying a crop, so I gave him little presses with my legs and little kicks with my heels, and then because I did that, I had to hold the reins a little more firmly. His neck arched some and I could feel his back sort of lift underneath me, and it was pretty clear we were going faster, though he didn't seem to be going faster. Abby sat for a minute in the middle of the arena, watching us, then called out, "Nice stride!" This meant that his steps were bigger. I stopped scowling. We went like this around the arena, then across the diagonal, then around the arena in the other direction, then across the diagonal again. When we came down to a halt, Abby said, "I never realized that Blue could be a dressage horse."

I said, "What is that?"

"Jane does it. It's like a square dance, where the horse does different kinds of steps in patterns. They have it in the Olympics."

"When do they jump?"

"They don't."

I trotted away to the far end of the arena, turned to the left, and asked Blue to canter. For the first time ever, he sort of leapt forward and I had to grab mane to keep my seat, and then he galloped in a very Gee Whiz sort of way all around the arena and back to where we took off. I got used to it. I gave myself instructions—sit deep, thumbs up, heels down, look ahead. Best of all, Blue seemed to like it, and once we came back to the walk, I wondered if he is bored all the time, too, because he's always very good and does what he is told.

Gee Whiz said, "He is not bored, he is boring." I turned as we passed Gee Whiz and stuck my tongue out at him. That made me laugh, and so now I was back in a good mood. I cantered Blue the other direction, and then Abby warmed up Gee Whiz while Blue and I walked here and there. I petted him down his neck, along his mane, and gave him a sugar cube. He flicked his ears and looked around. Now that his summer coat had grown in, he was almost white, only dappled just above his tail and down his legs. That's what happens to a gray horse as it grows up. The other thing is that he used to have a little blaze, but since his face is white, you can't see that, either.

The jumps were still set up the way they'd been the week before, and we did the same courses, but this time we did them going the other direction. Now that I was in a good mood again, I noticed that the wind was still blowing, especially across the green grass of the hillside, but Blue didn't seem to care anymore. The horses in the pasture, including Ned and Ben, were pretty excited—from time to time, they threw up their heads and ran from one spot to another, not as though they were escaping something, but as though they just wanted to do it. When Blue and I were walking around while Abby did some figure eights, Ned and Ben had a little race, maybe a hundred yards. Ben was winning by a neck, but Ned passed him. Then they bucked and played for a minute, walked around, and went back to the last of the hay. It reminded me of the paintings on the school for some reason—made me think that Ralphie and his friends were just having fun and almost (*almost*) didn't realize that they were doing a bad thing. I sat deep, looked up, kept my thumbs up, thought about my courses, and did all my jumping as well as the week before, only a little bit faster. Blue seemed to enjoy it more, too. He didn't touch a pole, or wander even a step, and his ears were pricked the whole time. After the third course, which was the spiral, Abby said, "Okay, I want you to do one little thing. Watch me again."

I had watched her do the spiral in a long, easygoing way, which seemed to suit Gee Whiz, because he has long legs and a long body, which is maybe the reason he was a good racehorse. But now she tightened the spiral so that even though they weren't going any faster, they were taking fewer steps and making shorter corners. Abby was sitting up straighter and Gee Whiz was paying close attention. When they were done, she said, "I think you can do that. Do you?"

Gee Whiz said, "No."

Blue once again didn't say anything.

I said, "I think so."

"Well, legs tight, elbows loose, watch where you are going." I nodded and did the first little circle to the right, then we were off.

Because the spiral was in the arena with other jumps, in order to complete the spiral, I had to decide how to get around the other jumps. The thing I saw Abby do was go inside rather than outside a few of them. That changed her course. After Blue and I went over the first jump, I did what Abby had done, which was to look to the right instead of to the left of the jump that was between us and our next one, and when I did that, Blue tightened his pace and turned a little bit—past that one and then in a curve to our second jump. Normally, you try to go straight to a jump, straight over it and straight away, but Blue could bend and jump at the same time. He did it with spring and I looked for the next obstacle. Here is a thing I know— the first jump sets you up for the next one and so on and so on, so if you know what you are doing, it gets easier, and if you are confused, it gets harder. There was nothing between the second and third jumps, but I shaved just a little bit off the curve—let's say that it went from being part of a circle to being part of an oval—and Blue turned neatly a stride before the fence and jumped straight. I felt my body sort of swing out, but the only thing that happened was that my left heel went down a little more. We cantered on.

Now there was a panel between the coop we had jumped and the hog's back we were going to jump—it was right in the way, like a colorful wall. The previous time I had gone around it without even thinking about it, but this time we were heading straight for it. I sat up, looked to the right, and tightened my hands on the reins. Blue switched leads (a flying change!) and went neatly past the panel and toward the hog's back. We jumped it and kept curving. I saw that even the rather open track for the last two was tighter than it had been. And I did see it—I saw it as if it were a road running through some grass—and I followed it, and we went over the jumps, cantered along the rail, and came down to the trot.

Abby was laughing and clapping. Gee Whiz had his ears pricked and looked friendly for once in his life, and when I loosened the reins, Blue arched his neck downward and pranced a few steps. I think maybe that was the best thing I ever did in my whole life, better than every A I ever got on a test, better than my walk around town, and better than Christmas and Easter combined. It was like a feeling of "joy to the world" all through my body as we came down to the walk and I took a few deep breaths. Even when that feeling began to go away, I knew that I would never forget it.

Chapter 17

Our lesson was one of those things that seem to take a long time, but when you look at the clock, you realize that they didn't. I think that's a weird thing about time, and I do not understand it. It comes and goes in waves, and sometimes the waves that seem big are small and the waves that seem small you can remember for days or weeks or months.

We walked the horses—no trail ride today, too windy still, though the sun was out more now—then we went back to the barn, untacked them, and put them into the pasture. Abby pointed toward Ned, and said there was plenty of time and that even though the jumping chute had been taken down, we ought to play with him a little in the round corral.

The round corral is between the arena and Abby's house. We were still alone. My dad hadn't come back, and Abby's dad's truck and her mom's car were still gone. Rusty was sitting on the front porch in the sunshine, with her tongue hanging out like she had been doing something exhausting, but we didn't know what it was. There are plenty of dogs in our town, but except when they go to the beach, they are always on leashes, walking along nicely. I could not imagine Abby's dog living like that.

Ned seemed happy, but he didn't have anything to say. I leaned on the fence while Abby stood in the center of the round corral and sent Ned around, to the left, to the right, walk, trot, canter. He did everything she said—she hardly had to use the long whip, just lift it when she wanted him to pick up speed and lower it when she wanted him to slow down. When she'd been doing this for a while, she dropped the whip completely, and Ned stopped and turned toward her. She said to me, "You want to try this?"

Of course I did, and so I got another lesson for the day, just a short one. She showed me how to lift the whip toward Ned's haunches to get him to go forward, then to take a little step toward his head to get him to slow down. To get him to come toward me, I was to step backward and turn away from him, and to get him to move away from me, I was to step straight toward him. My job was not to scare him, but to use my body to instruct him.

"Just tell me what to do," said Ned, but Abby was watching, and I didn't dare do anything that she might think was crazy, like talk to Ned. I did what she did. He went both ways, then Abby leaned down and whispered, "I'm going in the house for a minute."

Well, of course I knew she was going to the bathroom. This is another thing I don't understand, why you can't just say you're going to the bathroom. She walked out of the round corral with the whip, toward the house. I decided that I was tired, and went over and climbed on the fence, since there weren't any chairs anywhere. Now it was pretty hot, and I felt like Rusty must have felt, and I wished I could pant and let my tongue hang out of my mouth. Ned walked around, nosing for bits of whatever it is that he's always looking for.

After a while, he came over to me. He shivered all over, maybe because there were some flies around, even in the wind, and then he yawned and shook his ears. He said, "After you leave, I am going to take a nap."

I said, "After I leave, I am going to take a nap, too."

He stood right next to me and I tickled him in all those places that horses like to be tickled—around the eyes, down the neck, under the mane. His coat was warm, shiny, and soft. My hand just ran over it by itself, it felt so good. Now I yawned. Ned blew some air out of his nose. I said, "Were you up late last night?"

"That coyote came back. It was walking around the pasture."

"Is that scary?"

"It makes you pay attention. But Gee Whiz ran it off."

"He did?"

"He always does. He ran off a cougar when I first got here. He saw it and chased it and kicked it and it ran up the hill."

"Is he afraid of anything?"

"He's afraid of a couple of the mares."

I kept stroking his face. Abby didn't show up. Ned sighed.

I sighed.

That was when the idea came to me.

As soon as it did, I looked toward the house. Doors closed, no cars, everything quiet. And the wind had died. It seemed like the easiest thing in the world to do, and the very thing I wanted to do no matter what anyone else might think.

I said, "I'm going to get on you."

"Like a jockey?"

"Yup."

Ned stood there.

I said, "You have to be nice."

I looked around. The mares were over the hill in the mare pasture—couldn't see them. We were too far from the gelding pasture for Gee Whiz to say anything.

I stood up on the third rail and held the top rail, then I inched along, and when I got next to Ned's shoulder, I took my right hand and my right foot off the rail, then bent my left knee and slid onto Ned's back. I realized that I hadn't ridden bareback before—it was much different, both warmer and more slippery. Now I was sitting there, looking through Ned's ears. I put my hands in his mane and he started walking forward. He didn't seem excited but I could feel the energy in him, quite like the energy I had felt that morning in Blue, coming up from him into me. One step. Two three four five steps. He was very light on his feet. I looked toward the house again—still nothing. Six seven eight nine ten steps. No bridle, so no way to tell him what to do. We did what he wanted, which was to amble here and there. Twice he put his nose down, as if there might be some bit of grass in the dirt.

I looked at the house again. The door began to open, and I thought, *"Uh-oh,"* but then the phone rang—I could just barely hear it—and the door didn't open any farther. Four more steps, then I leaned forward, put my arms around Ned's neck, and slid off of him. I landed in a sort of stumbly way, but I'd regained my balance and was leaning against the fence when Abby appeared on the porch, her mouth wide. Then she came running. She didn't even close the door behind her.

She said, "He was second! He was second and he won a thousand dollars! And he's completely okay! I didn't even realize how afraid I was that something might happen until the trainer said he was good and happy and seemed to like it. Oh my!" And she put her face in her hands.

I said, "Are you crying?"

She let out a big breath and said, "Not yet."

I said, "Can you change his name to So Far So Good?"

Abby laughed out loud and gave me a hug, then we all were quiet for a long time, Abby, Ned, and me. The sun was out now—the clouds had skidded off to the east—and you could hear the birds cheeping and calling in the trees. All three of us, I knew, including Ned, were as happy as we could be. And then regular life started up again. Abby's dad pulled in, and Abby ran to the truck, then her mom came around the house and said that my dad was here, too, and then Dad said that we had to get home, because there was lots of traffic, and only an hour and a half till post time. He really did want to watch the race, and he clapped Abby on the back when she told him about Jack So Far, and then Gee Whiz whinnied from the pasture that he had won seven races out of sixty starts, ten places, three shows, way over a hundred thousand dollars. . . . Ned gave a snort, and if a horse can roll his eyes, he rolled his eyes.

Dad did ask me if I'd had a good time, and he did help me find all my stuff and get into the car, and he did congratulate Abby again about Jack getting second in his race, and he was careful to look behind when we backed out and to stop at every stop sign and red light. But he was in a hurry. He didn't care whether I talked or looked out the window, and so I looked out the window, and I remembered two things—sitting on Ned, step step step, mostly that moment when I realized that he wasn't going to do a single bad thing, and that second turn on Blue, in front of the colorful panel and straight to the hog's back. That's when I learned my lesson, and my lesson was that you always remember what you do much better than you remember what people say about it, even if they are really really happy for you and think you did a wonderful job.

Mom had the tuna fish sandwiches ready for a late lunch when we came in the house, and she was carrying Joan Ariel around just like it was the world's easiest thing to do. I kissed Joan Ariel on the cheek and Dad kissed her on the top of the head before he turned on the TV. The show about the Kentucky Derby was just beginning.

Dad watches sports—lots of baseball and some football—and even though I don't watch, I do walk past the TV from time to time and look at it, but in my whole life, I had never seen more people in one place than there were at the place where that horse race was. Mom let us eat our sandwiches and some potato chips right in front of the TV, and I sat there staring, trying to imagine Ned and Ben and Gee Whiz in a place like that. The announcers kept talking, and here came the horses with their jockeys, walking out onto the track, and there were a lot of other people with them—the horses were sort of alert and two or three of them kept looking around. One of them toward the back of the line trotted forward, not like he intended to buck and run away, but only like he *could* buck and run away. They walked and walked until they got to a long white thing called the starting gate, and some men led them into their stalls a few at a time, and then there was total silence, and then— *bam!*—the doors opened, and here they came, all dark in the sunshine. They looked small against the flatness of the racetrack. They ran toward the camera and then away, and you could see them go around a big oval, and then there they were on the other side of a huge crowd, running and running. I couldn't tell them apart, but some people could, because the announcer was saying who was in front and who was behind, and how many lengths and everything. Dad just sat there. I looked at him. He had a potato chip in his hand about three inches in front of his chin. Mom and Joan Ariel stood in the doorway.

Now the camera switched again, and the horses were running toward it. They looked pretty tired to me, but they knew what they were doing. One horse crossed the finish line, then two more crossed it almost together, and then a few more. The horse that won was number seven. Dad put his potato chip in his mouth and crunched it. Then he had a big grin all over his face and Mom said, "Did you bet on that horse?"

Dad said, "Only in my mind, but yeah, I thought he would win."

He jumped up and danced around the room, and then he held out his hands to me, and I danced around the room with him, and then Mom, very gently, began swaying Joan Ariel back and forth in her arms, so we were all dancing, and it had been a wonderful day.

Turn the page for a sneak peek at **ELLEN & NED**'s next adventure!

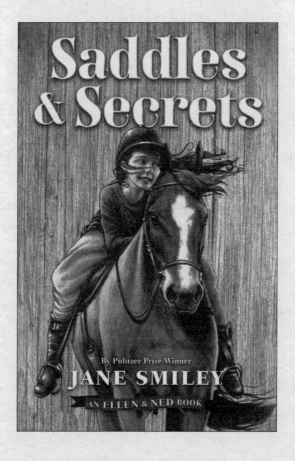

Saddles & Secrets

By Pulitzer Prize Winner

JANE SMILEY

AN ELLEN & NED BOOK

Chapter 1

After my lesson at Abby's ranch on Sissy, who is not as bad as she was in the spring, and can now even jump a little bit, Abby said that I had to learn something new, and I was sort of excited, but then the thing I was to learn was how to clean my saddle. I had to carry my own saddle into the tack room and put it on the saddle rack (I groaned a little so that Abby would know that the saddle was heavy, but she just laughed and handed me a sponge and a piece of soap that was blond and didn't smell anything like flowers). I watched her and did what she did—rubbed the sponge on the soap and then on the saddle and then on the soap and then on the saddle. She was fast. I was slow. And okay, I did close my eyes and let my mouth hang open a little so that she would think I was falling asleep, because one of the best ways to get through something boring is to make jokes.

While my eyes were closed, I thought maybe I really had fallen asleep, because I heard something I had never heard before, a deep, melodious voice singing, "From this valley they say you are going. We will miss your bright eyes and sweet smile." My eyes popped open, and I looked right at Abby, who didn't seem to hear a thing. The song went on, "For they say you are taking the sunshine that has brightened our pathway awhile."

Abby kept soaping.

I did, too. I listened to the end, and afterward there was silence, except for the soap soap soap. I finally said, "Did you hear something?"

"What?"

"A sad song."

"Oh, sure. 'Red River Valley.' That's one of his favorites."

"Who?"

"My dad. If he's in a good mood, he sings a sad song."

I said, "I never heard him sing before."

"Really?" She did not seem impressed. To me, it sounded like having a radio in your own barn. After a minute or so, she said, "He likes singing in the barn because the acoustics are good."

"What does that mean?"

"The walls and the ceiling make his songs sound richer."

"Don't you like it?"

"I do, but I hear it all the time."

Excerpt copyright © 2019 by Jane Smiley.
Published by Alfred A. Knopf, an imprint of Random House Children's Books, a division of Penguin Random House LLC, New York.